HARRY BANNER IN......

THE
CHRISTMAS
CARD KILLER

Steve Horsfall

This novel is entirely a work of fiction. The names, characters and incidents portrayed in it are the work of the author's imagination. Any resemblance to actual persons, living or dead, events or localities is entirely coincidental.

Cover Art: **SJH**

1

I walked at a brisk pace, eager to get back to the office and out of the cold. It was only six in the evening but the streets were quiet, with just a few other pedestrians scurrying by and there was very little traffic. The only sound was the faint beat of music from a nearby pub that was nearly drowned out by the newspaper seller on the corner.

"Southbury Echo," he yelled in a strained voice. "Read all about it. The Christmas Card Killer strikes again."

I would have normally passed straight by but instinctively held up a hand to beckon the seller to hand me a paper. I threw him a penny in exchange and moved into a shop doorway to shelter from the persistent drizzle and use the light to read the front page.

Third Victim for the Christmas Card Killer

Southbury is gripped by fear tonight as it was revealed that the fiend known as the Christmas Card Killer has struck again. The body of retired teacher, Lily Hutchins aged 65, was discovered by a neighbour this morning. She was found lying on her back with her throat slit and her arms carefully positioned to hold a Christmas card to her chest. The identical circumstance of the previous two victims.

One week ago, the dead body of a market stall holder, Peter Freeman aged 35, was found in an alley behind the Red Lion public house. This followed on from the first killing on the 1st December when a district nurse, Jill Smith aged 40, was killed on her rounds. Jill Smith's body was left under a hedge on Court Lane, with her bicycle placed against a nearby tree. Both victims had their throats slit from ear to ear. Both victims were left clutching a Christmas card, placed in their hands by the killer when they were already deceased.

The police confirmed tonight that no link can be found between the three known victims and that these killings appear to have been committed completely at random.

Inspector McAldren of Southbury Police told the Southbury Echo, 'We are asking for members of the public to be vigilant at this time and to take extra care when walking in the evening and to lock all doors and windows at night. If anyone should have any information or suspicions in regard to the killings, I urge them to contact Southbury Police station at their earliest convenience. I promise you we will catch this fiend and he will serve justice for his hideous crimes'.

"Sounds like some horrible freak, don't you think?" the Seller shouted over to me. "Southbury's very own Jack the Ripper."

I nodded as I folded the paper under my arm, "let's hope they find the killer soon."

Something dark crossed the man's face, "mark my words there'll be more bodies to come and with Christmas only two weeks away. Never sold so many papers though, so every cloud and all that"

I looked over at him, "if you know anything, you should talk to Inspector McAldren."

"Only joking mate," the Seller held up his hands. "Although can't say I have much confidence in that McAldren bringing him in."

I moved out of the doorway, "that's assuming that our killer is a he."

The Seller took a breath and gave me a curious stare as I walked back out into the dusk. It was only when I had crossed the road that he shouted out to a group of passers-by.

"Read all about it. The Christmas Card Killer strikes again."

2

The morning.

I sat at my desk sorting through a pile of paperwork, stopping frequently to sip from a cup of extremely bitter black coffee. There was a mix of bills, bank statements and quite a few letters requesting my services as a Private Investigator. I paused briefly on each letter but could tell within a few lines that they were not cases I cared to take on. Lots of missing pets, an old widow who was convinced her dearly departed husband was still alive and living with his fancy woman down the road, and a young man who wanted someone to look for an engagement ring he had dropped in a field on his way to getting down on one knee.

I was easily distracted from my mundane task, picking up the Southbury Echo I had bought the previous evening and reading through the front-page story once again. I sat back trying to digest it all. Could the so-called Christmas Card Killer really just be a random murderer? I had seen other reports calling the killer Southbury's very own Jack the Ripper, echoing the thoughts of the Echo seller from last night, but even that beast had an obvious motive in wanting to kill. His prey was prostitutes; the victims of the Christmas Card Killer supposedly had no common connection at all.

I picked up the cup of now stewed, cold coffee and headed for the kitchen to make a fresh cup. I had hardly got halfway across the office when there was a loud knock on the front door. Through the frosted glass I could see the silhouettes of two men; I could already tell who one of my visitors was from the distinct outline of his oversized coat, and just by the way he was standing.

When I opened the door and prepared to greet my guests, Inspector McAldren just walked straight on in without so much as a word. He was wearing the infamous khaki trench coat. His companion stood in the doorway and threw me a smile. He was short and stocky with a mop of black curly hair and was wearing an expensive grey suit under his suave black camel hair coat. He looked familiar.

"Hello Mister Banner," he said. "It's nice to meet you." He held out a hand which I promptly shook.

I frowned, "sorry have we met before?"

He shook his head. "Not to my knowledge. My name is Martin Warburton"

"Mayor Warburton," I quickly interjected.

"Took your time Banner," McAldren shouted from inside the office, where he had already taken a seat at my desk. His receding brown hair was slicked back with even more oil than usual and he looked more like a tramp with thick stubble around his jawline.

I beckoned for Warburton to come in and after hesitating he stepped tentatively into the office. I took his coat and offered him a chair next to McAldren. The Inspector brushed away my half-hearted attempt to take his mangy old coat. I swear that he probably slept in it.

As Warburton sat down I observed how tired he looked. Nothing like the pristine image that was portrayed in the press. His face was also covered in dark stubble as if he had not shaved for a few days; the top button of his shirt was undone and a badly knotted tie hung loose. His whole demeanour was full of fret.

"Please, gentlemen, to what do I owe this pleasure?" I asked as I took my place on the other side of the desk.

McAldren looked sceptical. "Believe me this is not a pleasure Banner, but the Mayor has a notion that you may be of some assistance."

Warburton sat quietly, nervously studying his surroundings.

"So Mayor," McAldren continued. "Would you like to explain your bright idea?"

Warburton said, "Please McAldren, there is no need to get hostile."

McAldren confirmed the obvious. "Can't say I like the idea at all."

I sat forward and smiled. "I guess you better tell me what you have in mind."

Warburton nodded as he reached for the copy of the Southbury Echo on my desk. He held up the front page and pointed to the **Christmas Card Killer** headline. "We need your help to catch this beast before he kills again." His voice cracked with emotion.

I just nodded, thinking for a moment.

"Take your time Banner," McAldren urged.

"Wait a minute." I angled a smile at McAldren. "Is this because the police are stumped?"

McAldren shrugged.

Warburton inhaled deeply. "I would deny it if ever asked in public, but stumped sort of sums it up."

"We'll get him eventually," McAldren countered. "Always do."

Warburton rubbed his eyes, "the trouble is we do not have time Mister Banner. This killer is striking at will and we have no leads whatsoever. Southbury is living in fear as nobody can be sure that they will not be the next victim. Our killer is running rings around everyone."

I looked at McAldren again. "Will I be expected to work with the police or can I run it my way?"

McAldren widened his eyes but held his tongue.

Warburton hesitated, thinking. "You can run it your way but all I ask is you keep McAldren appraised of what you're doing and if you get any major leads. You'll be well paid for your time whether you catch him or the police do."

McAldren winced, "you'd better not hold anything back from me Banner or all bets are off."

I studied McAldren for a few seconds, nodded and looked back at Warburton. "What are you offering?"

Warburton picked up a sheet of paper and a pen. He wrote on the paper, folded it and pushed it towards me. I picked up the sheet and opened it slowly, rubbing my chin as I looked at the number, before folding once more and putting the note in my shirt pocket. I winked at McAldren.

"Do we have a deal?" Warburton asked

"We do," I replied.

Warburton stood and offered me his hand once more, which I promptly shook again.

McAldren leaned back in the chair, considering a comment but said nothing. Instead he stood up and made his way towards the door.

"We will expect you at Southbury Police station this morning," Warburton said sternly. "McAldren will fill you in on what we know. You will be provided with all the resources you need."

"Yeah, whatever." McAldren dismissed me with a hand wave. He opened the door and waited for Warburton.

Warburton turned to go before looking back with one final comment. "I hear you're the best Banner. I really hope that is true."

I looked straight at him. "I won't let you down."

Once my visitors had gone, I pulled out my beloved Lafayette trumpet. I gave it a blast, celebrating the fact that a paycheque of two hundred pounds was coming my way. For a moment I could revel in my wealth before getting down to business and solving the case of the Christmas Card Killer.

I played *The Santa Claus Express.*

3

I took a ride on the tram into the town centre from where it was a short walk to Southbury Police station. McAldren was waiting for me by the front desk at the station, stood tall in his khaki trench coat. The duty sergeant did not look too pleased to have company as the Inspector puffed tirelessly on a cigarette, producing plumes of thick rancid smoke. McAldren always bought cheap, low quality, cigarettes.

McAldren glared at me. "What kept you Banner?"

I shrugged. "Didn't know I had to clock-in. Hope you're not going to dock my pay."

The sergeant smirked as he wrote something down in a logbook.

McAldren shook his head. "Follow me." He turned on his heels and headed into the station. I exchanged knowing smiles with the sergeant before slowly following behind.

I was led to a small office, where McAldren duly barged in without knocking. An incredibly young skinny policeman in full uniform was sat at a desk strewn with paper. He twitched nervously at the sight of McAldren.

"Take a break now Kane." McAldren approached the desk and picked up a folder.

"Thank you sir," Kane replied timidly

"Go and rustle up some tea and be back in ten minutes," McAldren snorted.

As Kane left the room after a backward glance, McAldren handed me the folder. I opened it to find three sheets of paper filled with badly smudged writing.

I made a face. "Looks like some poorly written homework."

McAldren crossed the room and pulled across a couple of stacked chairs, scraping them loudly on the floor. He separated them and beckoned for me to sit. I did so as McAldren plonked himself down in the other.

McAldren studied me for a moment. "What you have in your hand is all we have Banner, so I suggest you read it very carefully."

I sat up and nodded. "Not sure I can read the childish writing."

"Yeah, whatever." McAldren dismissed me with a swish of his hand. "Kane will decipher for you. When he comes back with your char, the lad can talk you through all the finer points."

I eyeballed him. "No wonder the Mayor wants to bring me in."

"Don't push it with me," McAldren rasped.
I tilted my head, "of course not sir."

McAldren's scowl did not change. "Earn what we're paying you and bring something to the table Banner. Prove to me that I'm wrong about this crazy arrangement."

Kane re-entered the room with impeccable timing. McAldren did not look up but carried on giving me the glare.

I decided to ease the situation with tact. "I think I need that tea now Kane. The Inspector tells me you are the man to bring me up to speed on the case." I placed the folder back on the table.

Kane smiled and place two white chipped cups on the table, nervously spilling some of the steaming tea on the folder in the process. I said nothing.

"Listen up Kane," McAldren snarled whilst pointing a finger at me. "Walk the so-called private detective here through all the facts we've gathered and see if he can come up with any bright ideas. Be professional at all times, as if you were presenting evidence in the dock. Do not sink to his level of flippancy and sarcasm. If you think he is undermining our work in any way, you are to report your concerns to me. Got it?"

The lad just stood there. He was tall and lanky with a short back and sides haircut and a smooth face that looked like it had never been shaved.

"Got that Kane?" McAldren repeated.

"Yes sir," Kane replied, although he looked on blankly.

McAldren stood up to go, still giving me the glare. I checked my watch as if making a point. The Inspector made a face but did not take the bait. He left the room, slamming the door as he went.

I gave a quick whistle. "He must be a joy to work for Kane?"

Kane just nodded and sat down. He picked up his tea and started sorting through the very slim crime file.

I sat back and said nothing.

Kane swallowed, "how would you like to proceed sir?"

I shrugged, "maybe from the beginning and don't ever call me sir again."

Kane looked up, puzzled.

"Call me Harry," I confirmed.

Kane nodded.

"So," I continued. "Tell me all about the first murder."

Kane folded his arms across his chest and sighed. "We were convinced the first killing was by a deranged admirer. Jill Smith was a very attractive lady who frequently attracted male attention as she cycled on her rounds as a district nurse. We heard a lot of stories about Miss Smith being heralded by wolf whistles as she rode past the East Side building site and that a number of men would enquire about taking her out for the evening. She was, however, a spinster who lived alone."

I nodded. "Do we know if Miss Smith took up any of these offers?"

Kane made a face. "Not according to any witnesses we spoke to and Miss Smith did not seem to have any close friends. Although a couple of her colleagues were convinced that she was having an affair with a married man that had been going on for several years. One neighbour did report seeing a male visitor to Miss Smith's house on numerous occasions. He was described as being around fifty years old with silver grey hair and a moustache to match. He was also described as being very dapper, wearing expensive suits and always a cravat."

"Interesting." I thought for a moment. "I assume that this mystery gentleman has not been traced?"

"Precisely," Kane replied. "To be honest, we stopped looking once the other murders took place. He was suspect number one when we just had one killing but it made no sense that he would then go after other random strangers after that."

I tilted back in my chair and smiled. "He might not be our killer but he could provide invaluable information as to why our first victim was selected. It is always the first victim that holds the key. Tell me about how Miss Smith was found."

Kane referred to his notes. "The body was found lodged under a hedge by a man walking his dog. It was the dog that alerted the owner after the mutt starting burrowing next to the body. Death was caused by one precise slash across the throat with a very sharp knife. The attacker struck from behind the victim."

I nodded. "According to the press, the body was placed neatly with the arms folded and the Christmas card placed in the victim's hand."

Kane looked up at me. "That's correct and of course it made no sense at all at the time."

"Was there anything written in the card?" I asked.

"Yes," Kane answered. "The words 'number one' had been inscribed."

I raised an eyebrow, "I guess that was kept from the press?"

Kane nodded.

"Soooo," I said, stretching the word out, "it would appear that you made no progress at all in the investigation of the first murder and then bam! Murder number two."

Kane sipped his tea and pondered for a moment. "It was assumed that the first murder was a crime of passion but when our second victim was reported it is fair to say that there was general mood of bewilderment."

I raised an eyebrow. "So tell me about the market stall holder."

"Peter Freeman was by all accounts a chirpy character who was liked by everyone who met him. He ran a fruit and veg stall near the Guild Hall and was well known for his cheeky sales patter and charm with all his regular customers." Kane paused and sat back, rubbing his tired eyes.

I shifted in my seat a little. "How was he killed?"
Kane sighed. "Same as Jill Smith. One sharp knife cut to the throat from behind. It seems that the killer struck after Freeman left the Red Lion pub, where he had enjoyed a few pints of beer with some friends. He was apparently in exceptionally good spirits when he left the pub, but a little unsteady on his feet."

I leaned closer. "Sounds like our killer was waiting for him outside but the question is was it a random attack or was Freeman always the intended victim?"

"We just don't know the answer," Kane confirmed. "It would appear that Freeman and Jill Smith have never actually met and have no mutual friends whatsoever."

"What about the placing of the body?" I asked.

Kane smiled. "Freeman was placed exactly like Jill Smith. The body was placed neatly with the arms folded and the Christmas card placed in the victim's hand. There was no effort to obscure the body. Freeman was placed in the middle of the alley that runs behind the pub and was discovered within hours of the attack by a young couple."

I leaned back. "Did anyone in the pub spot any strangers hanging around? Any of Freeman's friends confirm why he might have been attacked?"

Kane shook his head. "No on both counts. The pub was full of regulars and no strangers seen outside. Freeman's friends were totally shocked that he was the victim. As I say, exceedingly popular character."

I pondered. "Did Freeman have a wife, girlfriend or lover?"

Kane shrugged. "Not married and had apparently been single for over a year after splitting with his previous girlfriend."

"Seems drastic," I mused. "Have you spoken to the ex-girlfriend?"

Kane looked up at me, "she's dead. Died last Christmas in a road accident a few months after splitting with Freeman. Knocked over by a tram on the high street. We pulled out the report as soon as Freeman's friends informed us."

"I see," I said in a quiet voice. "That must have hit Freeman hard?"

"Yes, very much apparently according to his friends," Kane confirmed.

"Any link with the former girlfriend and Jill Smith?" I asked.
"None," Kane replied.

"And the Christmas card left in Freeman's hand by the killer?" I enquired.

"Simply inscribed with the words 'number two'," Kane confirmed

"And what about our latest victim?" I pressed on.

"Lily Hutchins, a retired teacher who taught at St Mary's school for nearly forty years." Kane referred to the notes in the file.

"St Mary's is an all-girls grammar school," I affirmed.

"Correct," Kane replied.

I frowned. "Did Jill Smith attend that school?"

"No, she was educated up north somewhere." Kane replied. "We checked, hoping for a connection. Jill Smith only moved to Southbury around five years ago."

I pulled the file over and read through the notes once more as Kane stayed silent.

I shook my head. "I just don't buy into the fact that someone is going around randomly killing people. There has to be a connection with all three victims."

"What do you think that connection is?" Kane asked.

I frowned. "I have absolutely no idea."

The phone rang out loudly and Kane answered it immediately.

"Yes sir, I'll bring him down pronto," was all Kane muttered into the mouthpiece before hanging up.

I looked at Kane as he stood.

"I am to take you down to one of the interview rooms," Kane said. "It would seem that Inspector McAldren has arrested a prime suspect."

4

Kane led the way down a long corridor. McAldren was waiting by the door to the interview room, looking like the cat who had got the cream.

McAldren snapped his fingers and pointed at me, smirking for all his worth. "In the time you've been drinking tea and reading a report Banner, I've been out doing real police work. I think we may have our man."

"Impressive," I remarked with a smile. "I really hope you do have him."

"He's in there," McAldren nodded at the door.

I opened the door slightly and peered in. A scruffy man in a threadbare brown suit sat staring into space. He had a mop of unkempt ginger hair and a matted grey beard. The man began twitching and was muttering incoherently to himself, sniggering as he did so. I closed the door again.

I turned and looked at McAldren. "Seriously?"

McAldren considered for a moment. "He was reported by one of my constables to have been at the scene of all three murders. When approached by the constable at the Lily Hutchins' murder scene, he shouted 'you've got me; I knew my luck wouldn't last'. He keeps repeating over and over 'how did you know how to find me?'"

I wasn't buying it. "This does not sound right. It just doesn't." My voice faded away.

McAldren snorted. "Sometimes, in fact most of the time, solving crimes is just a simple task. Old fashioned policing is all that is required."

I stared at him until McAldren finally opened the door and beckoned for me to join him in interviewing our prime suspect. Kane waited outside.

The suspect looked up and smiled at me. He was missing a few teeth.

"Mr Greene, this is Harry Banner, a Private Detective who has been helping the police to investigate the Christmas Card killings." McAldren scoffed.

"How do you do sir," the suspect spoke with a very posh tone as he offered me his hand. "I am Simon Greene."

I nodded and sat alongside McAldren.

"Why did you do it Simon?" McAldren snarled.

He said nothing, but just looked down at the desk, his eyes full of shame.

"What did these people ever do to you?" McAldren continued.

"I ....I loved her." Greene replied, still looking down.

"Who did you love?" I asked

"My dearly beloved wife," Greene began to sob.

I glanced sideways at McAldren.

"I killed her because I could no longer trust her," Greene rambled on.

"Who did you kill Simon?" I asked softly.

"The two of them," he confirmed.

"You mean three?" McAldren interjected.
"Did I kill three people?" Greene finally looked up. "I was so taken with rage that I cannot recall so clearly."

"Why did you leave the Christmas Cards with your victims Greene?" McAldren pressed on, eager to close the case by lunch.

"I do not know," Greene mumbled.

"How did you kill them Simon?" I asked.

"With an axe," Greene broke down and cried hysterically.

"An axe?" I repeated. "Who did you kill Simon?"

Greene kept his eyes to the desk. "My wife and that Philanderer, Martin Kilblane."

"When did you kill them Simon?" I asked.

He raised his head meekly. "It would be some twenty years ago."

McAldren opened a file and pushed some photographs across the table. They showed all three victims as they were found in death: all clutching Christmas cards with very similar plain designs.

"Take a look Simon," McAldren said after he had finished shuffling the photos in front of his prime suspect.

Simon looked puzzled. "I think these are the bodies I have seen on the street. Whatever happened to them?"

McAldren leaned toward Greene. "You killed them Simon," he snarled.
Greene spread his hands wide. "I can assure you I did not. I do not even know them."

I angled a smile at McAldren and then at Greene. "Simon, why did you happen to see all of these bodies?"

Greene shrugged. "I live on the streets and spend my days wandering to find food and warmth. If I see a crowd gathered and the police in attendance, I will stop to take a look. Such things provide something interesting or exciting in my pitiful life."

McAldren made a face. "Are you telling me that you were just hanging around like some ghoul?"

"Pretty much," he replied. "Part of me always wants to test to see if the police will still recognise me after all these years, and today that finally happened."

I gave a quick whistle. "Very Impressive McAldren. Looks like you've cracked the case, but just not the one you are working on."

Something dark crossed McAldren's face. He stood up and left the room, slamming the door hard behind him.

Greene took out a dirty handkerchief and blew his nose before giving me a nervous sideway glance.

"Tell me Simon," I said. "When you were hanging around the different places where the bodies were found, did you spot anything unusual?"

"How do you mean?" Green asked

"Well did you see anybody acting unusually," I explained.
Greene squinted badly. "Not really. Most of the crowds were simply curious, and a quite a few seemed worried that they may be murdered too."

I nodded. "So you did not speak to anyone in any of the crowds?"

Greene lifted his head up and looked at me. "I spoke to a young policeman on all three occasions and I think it was he who must have recognised me. A vile fugitive from justice."

"I see," I muttered whilst checking the clock on the far wall and wondering how long McAldren would be.

Green let loose a deep breath. "Oh wait, I did try and console a man at the scene of the first killing. He was sobbing gently and I could tell the lady meant a lot to him."

"Go on," I said

"Well, I just asked if he was alright," Greene continued. "He looked at me as if I had caught him out and hot tailed it off down the road."

"What did he look like?" I asked

Greene thought for a moment. "Grey hair and a moustache. He wore a long grey coat and a bright red cravat."

Greene had just described Jill Smith's supposed lover to a tee.

The door flew open and McAldren marched in. "Well Greene, I've got good news and bad news," he snapped.

Greene glanced at me and then back at McAldren, just as a young uniformed constable entered the room.

"The good news is that you are in the clear for the Christmas Card murders," McAldren sneered. "A witness has come forward to say you were ensconced at the South Street hostel on the two evenings when Peter Freeman and Lily Hutchins were killed."

Greene sat up. "Does that mean I am free to go?"

"And the bad news?" I interjected.

McAldren grunted. "It seems that there is still an open case for the murder of Phyllis Greene and Martin Kilblane." He turned to the young officer, "take this pile of filth down to the cells constable."

This whole façade was over. Green was led away by the constable, with McAldren hot on their heels. It would seem that the Inspector was not too keen to face me right now.

I ambled out of the room to find Kane still waiting. "One to cross off the list," he remarked.

"Not sure he should have ever been on the list," I said.

"What will you do next?" Kane asked.

"Always start with the first victim," I replied. "We shall go to where Jill Smith met her sticky end."

5

Thirty minutes later I was outside Jill Smith's house. It was a grey mid-terrace two-up two-down with a relatively long garden at the front. Kane stood alongside me. McAldren had made it clear that Kane worked with me or the deal was off. I insisted that Kane changed into plain clothes and did the driving; they let him take out an unmarked black Hillman.

"Nice place," Kane commented. "She owned it too. Paid it off a couple of years ago."

"How much do they pay nurses these days?" I asked jokingly

"No clue," Kane replied. "You think she had a benefactor?"

I fixed him with the big eyes. "The dapper boyfriend perhaps."

I walked over and opened the garden gate and made my way up to the front door with Kane in tow. The garden path was uneven and badly cracked; the lawn and flower beds were overgrown with weeds. The young constable suddenly scurried past with a key in his hand. "I'll open up," he shouted.

I waited and watched as Kane took his time mastering the lock before finally swinging the dark oak door open. I followed Kane inside as he kicked aside a small pile of post on the floor. I immediately noticed how clean and well kept the hallway was. A long plush red rug ran the length of the hall; the walls were adorned with tasteful landscape paintings and a large ornate round gold mirror. There was a sweet aroma in the air, like an expensive perfume. The lounge was just the same; another plush red rug in front of a marble fireplace with a shiny brass front. More tasteful art dominated the walls and the chairs were expensive French regency.

I moved to the window and pulled the curtain aside. The garden was just so overgrown and not in keeping with the house at all.

Kane cleared his throat. "She certainly lived well."

I stayed silent and instead took a seat, looking up at a delicate French chandelier. "It is as if Miss Smith did not want to advertise her opulence as the garden is so badly kept that you would assume the house was the same. I certainly made that assumption."

Kane nodded. "Not one neighbour confirmed they had ever been in the house. It would seem that she took such pride in her home solely for her own pleasure"

"As well as her only reported visitor," I corrected.

"But sadly there is nothing here to connect us with this man," Kane almost sighed. "We have searched the whole house."

"There must be someway to find him," I returned. "Did Miss Smith leave a will?"

Kane hesitated for a second, "not exactly but the hospital where she worked claim they have documents that show the house being bequeathed in the event of Miss Smith's death to fund the hiring of more nurses. Nobody else has come forward so it seems that the hospital will at least gain from her death."

I raised an eyebrow, "I guess it would be difficult for her dapper male visitor to come forward if he is indeed married."

"Quite," Kane scoffed.

A sudden clattering noise from the hall made Kane visibly twitch as I leapt to my feet.

"Just the post," Kane shouted after me. I was already at the door. I pulled it open in time to see the postman as the end of the path.

"Hey," I shouted after him. "Can you spare me a few minutes."

The postman stopped and turned to look back at me, pushing up his peaked black cap as he did so. He was very tall and thin with a bushy black moustache. I aged him at around late thirties.

"Who are you sir?" he asked a little nervously.

I smiled. "I'm a detective looking into the death of the lady who lived here. I'm with Constable Kane from the Southbury Police force." Kane stepped into view by my side.

"I had nothing to do with it, I swear," the postman pleaded as he stepped forward, removing his cap to reveal a mop of black curly hair. "Besides, I hear the lady was found over a mile from here."

I walked down towards the postman. "I can confirm that you are certainly not a suspect."

The postman wiped his brow, looking relieved.

"They always say that if you want to know what goes on in any house, ask the postman," I continued.

The postman eyed me before giving a broad smile. "Ain't that the truth."

"My name is Harry Banner and as I mentioned this is Constable Kane," I beckoned Kane to my side. "And your name is?"

His eyes drifted a little. "Richard Jones," he finally answered with a mumble.

Just as he spoke a police car sped past, sirens screaming. It nearly made Jones jump out of his skin.

I smiled, "you really are nervous."

Jones shuffled forward. "It's all these stories about this Christmas Card Killer. The whole town is on edge."

I nodded. "Tell me Richard, did you ever see a frequent visitor to this house? A dapper dresser by all accounts with grey hair and a moustache."

Jones swallowed. "Yes, I spotted him on many occasions."
"Do you know anything about him?" I asked

"It is Lord McNair," Jones replied without hesitation. "I used to deliver to the McNair Manor out at Downsbury, a few miles down the road."

"Are you sure?" Kane interjected.

Jones laughed. "I'm positive. He would always sneak around, which made me laugh as he always stood out. I mean why would a Lord hang around this neighbourhood?"

We let Jones get on with his round after thanking him for his help.

Kane let loose a deep breath as we walked back to the car.

"What?" I asked.

"I'm just amazed at how lucky we were to get that lead," he chuckled whilst climbing into the driver's seat

"No luck involved," I confirmed, a little smugly, and lit up a cigarette. Kane said nothing but did wind down the window to show his distaste for the smoke filling the car.

6

McNair Manor was what they call a small country estate. The Manor was located at the far end of the village of Downsbury, set in around 30 acres of land. It only took around fifteen minutes to drive from Southbury. I had barely finished my cigarette.

You could see the house from the road as we drove out of the village, sitting on its own in the middle of the countryside. When we got to the entrance the gate was open and so I told Kane just to drive on in. We headed down a long gravel drive, flanked by a well-kept garden on each side. As we got out of the car I looked up at the three storey house, with rows of seven windows on the top two floors. How many rooms did these people need?"

"Can I help you gentlemen?" A very snooty butler appeared from the side of the house. He looked a little sheepish as he quickly stubbed out a cigarette with his foot.

Kane cleared his throat. "We're here to see Lord McNair."

The butler fixed us both with big eyes. "And who might you be?"

"Southbury Police," I announced, trying not to laugh. Kane gave me a disapproving look.

"I see," the butler pondered. "Do you have an appointment to see Lord McNair?"

"Don't be stupid, we're the police." I walked forward a little irritated

Kane remained silent but reached into his pocket and produced a police badge. The butler studied the badge for a moment before nodding his head to seemingly acknowledge we were telling the truth.

The butler cleared his throat. "Follow me."

He led the way into a wide hallway with a white marble floor. There was a staircase to the left, also marble but with a red carpet runner down the middle. A series of grand portraits adorned the walls. I assumed they were depicting a various assortment of toffs from the McNair family tree. To the right of the stairs was a long thin table that looked foreign. Maybe French. In the middle of the table stood a tall vase holding two long singular sunflowers. The butler quickly ushered Kane and I into a side room. As expected, the room was also exquisitely furnished with two plush velvet sedan chairs either side of a white grand piano. More paintings adorned the walls but this time they depicted animals; several horses, a couple of beagles and one large fox hunting scene hanging over the huge fireplace.

"Please wait here and do not touch anything," the butler said in gruff condescending voice. "I will collect Lord McNair presently. Can I have an indication of the nature of your visit?"

I shrugged. "Just mention the name, Jill Smith."

After a few seconds of silence the butler left the room, closing the door behind him.

I turned to Kane and smiled at him.

Kane did not smile. "Please don't go around claiming you're a police officer Harry. You'll get us both in trouble. McAldren will have my guts for garters."

I walked over to the piano. "I suppose I am an honorary policeman for the day, so got to make the most of it."

Kane arched a sceptical eyebrow but said nothing. I played a few notes of *Fur Elise*.

"You play," Kane remarked.

"A little," I replied and stopped. I had exhausted my entire repertoire. "More of a trumpet player."

"I knew that," Kane almost shouted. "Don't you play at Smooth's club occasionally?"

"The Blue Bay," I confirmed almost begrudgingly. The fact that local gangster Maxwell Gray, aka Smooth, was my employer did not sit well with me.

Right on cue the door flew open and a very flustered Lord McNair bounded into the room, carefully closing the door behind him. He stood for a moment, nervously stroking his silver moustache. He wore a light brown suit and a navy-blue cravat. This was our man.

"I really do not think I can help you gentlemen," he said without preamble. "I did not really know Jill Smith that well at all."

I shrugged. "Then it should not make any difference if we interview you with Lady McNair present. Just in case we need to confirm her as an alibi if required. Is her Ladyship home?"

He sighed deeply and moved closer. "Look, alright, I admit that Jill was a close acquaintance, but I really do not know why she was killed. I was devastated to hear the news."

"An acquaintance?" Kane chipped in.

"Alright, she was my lover," McNair snapped. This interview was not going to require any tough interrogation.

"And did you also know either Lily Hutchins or Peter Freeman?" Kane pressed on.

"No, not at all," McNair replied indignantly. "I am aware that Jill was a victim of this Christmas Card Killer and I have been keeping up to date on the news of the case. I know the two people you mention were also victims, but I have never set eyes on them."

"How was Jill Smith in the period leading up to her death?" I tried a different tact. "Did she act differently in any way?"

McNair sat down on one of the sedans. "Jill was nearly always very bubbly and full of life. She loved being a nurse but occasionally she would get upset if a patient died. I remember last Christmas when she tried unsuccessfully to save the life of a young woman in a road accident. That really upset her and this Christmas period brought back some bad memories. She even visited the young lady's grave and left flowers."

"Did you know the name of the young woman?" Kane asked

"Sorry, no," was the instant reply.

I nodded. "Did she mention anything else?"

McNair looked up at the ceiling and rested an index finger on his chin. "Well, I suppose there was the one thing."

I looked straight at him. "Go on."

"Jill was never short of male admirers." McNair said softly. "There was one man, a carpenter working near to Jill's house. He and his fellow builders were renovating that old butcher shop. Trenchards it was called. This carpenter took more than a fancy to Jill. He bombarded her with chocolates and flowers. At first she was flattered but then became convinced that someone was following her and watching her house."

"She thought it was this carpenter?" Kane asked.

"Yes, but she would not let me confront him?" McNair replied gruffly.

"Would also have been difficult with your predicament," I suggested. "A married man drawing attention to himself."

"Quite," McNair confirmed.

"How did you meet Jill and how long had this affair been going on?" I asked bluntly.

McNair hesitated. "Jill treated me for mild pneumonia about three years ago. She was a wonderful nurse and we seemed to have so much in common. I continued to meet with Jill after my treatment and we got on so well. One thing led to another and we became more than friends. But I also loved my wife and would never leave her for another."

"Was Jill Smith happy with this arrangement?" Kane asked.

"She was," McNair replied. "Although I did help her financially to sweeten the arrangement."

"The house?" I stated.
McNair nodded.

"You were spotted at the scene of Jill's murder." I commented. "Had you been with Jill at the time of her murder?"

"No, that evening I was here at the house hosting a dinner party and dance. It was a masked ball." McNair sighed. "I went to see Jill the next morning and stumbled on the murder scene."

"I assume you have a number of guests from the ball who can corroborate you story?" Kane asked officially.

"Of course," McNair conceded, "but please use the utmost discretion."

At that moment there was a knock at the door and woman walked into the room. Aged around mid-fifties, she was very thin with a pointed chin and a head of thick, beautifully coiffed, white hair. She wore a long green velvet dress.

"Rodney, who are these gentlemen?" she asked.

"Nothing to worry about my dear," McNair's voice was soft but slightly flustered.

Lady McNair looked daggers at her husband. "Naresby has informed me that they are from the police."

McNair said nothing.

"What's going on? What are you not telling me?" Her Ladyship stormed up to her husband.

McNair just tilted his head forward as if in disgrace.

"I'll ask one more time," she persisted. "Who are these men?"

I decided to help him out. "It is correct your Ladyship that we are investigating a police matter."

Her eyes flicked away from her husband and now she was training her scowl on me. "What kind of police matter?"

"We're investigating the death of a nurse by the name of Jill Smith," I confirmed. "The reason we wished to speak to you husband was that he was a former patient of Miss Smith. He has been extremely helpful."

She cocked her head. "How preposterous!"

"Just routine madam," Kane chipped in.

"And why are you not in uniform? What kind of policemen are you?" She continued, now with a wagging finger.

"The inconspicuous kind," I offered.

"Well, it is very irregular," she scowled. "I will be talking to your superiors. I happen to know Inspector McAldren very well."

"As you wish," I conceded as I stood. "Although Inspector McAldren is not actually my superior."

Now she was flummoxed.

Kane took the long silent pause as a time to get up from the chair. "Thank you for your time Lord McNair. You've been very helpful but we'll be on our way."

"Oh." McNair mumbled. "My pleasure. I hope you find the fiend."

"Thank you for your patience too your Ladyship," I bowed towards her.

She did not reply. The butler, Naresby showed us out and we could hear Lady McNair screaming the odds as we stepped out the front door.

"Easy to see why his Lordship strayed don't you think?" I smiled knowingly at Kane.

Kane said nothing but I'm sure I detected a smirk as we headed back to the car.

7

Kane drove back to Jill Smith's house and parked outside. We then walked across the road and down a small alleyway that led through a small crescent of four shops. A tailor, a cobbler, a baker and a butcher. The four premises were all connected in a Victorian terrace, with a cobbled path along the front. It was like going back in time. Trenchards, the butcher shop, had an elegant green tiled front wall, although the window was crudely boarded. We walked on down to the entrance to find the front door removed. We could hear a lot of banging and hammering coming from inside, and there were clouds of dust wafting into the street.

"I've only just had this suit cleaned," I moaned as I stepped inside. Kane followed.

There was even more dust inside the shop as two men in grey boiler suits smashed a central display cabinet with mallets. They were so engrossed in their work that we had to wait several minutes before the shorter of the two noticed we were there, although only short in comparison to his companion. He was a giant of a man, getting on towards seven foot, with wide shoulders and a bulky muscular frame. He had a thick black beard and a head of long curly hair. The shorter man had thin receding brown hair and a couple of scars across one cheek.

The room went still after Shortie slapped the Giant on his shoulder to get his attention. The Giant just stood there, his face expressionless.

"And who the hell are you just walking in here without invitation?" Shortie raged.

I put up my hands in mock surrender. "Easy lad, I'll let him tell you who we are." I nodded in Kane's direction.

Both men took a step forward, glaring at Kane.

Kane held up a badge, "we're from the Police."

The Giant spoke for the first time. "Just why would the police want to come and visit such honest hard-working men like us?" He had a slight Irish lilt.

"We heard that you have a carpenter on the firm," I stepped in. "We would like a quiet word with him."

The Giant looked amused, "you don't look like a policeman."

I shrugged, "let's just say I'm assisting the police on an important case."

Shortie shook his head, releasing a layer of dust in the process. "Well, it looks like your case has gone cold as there isn't any carpenter here."

"Okay," I said, remaining patient. "So where can we find him?"

The Giant stared at me. "We're a small outfit. Just me and him. If you want to find yourself a carpenter, I suggest you look elsewhere." He stepped forward menacingly.

Kane raised his hand. "I suggest you stay calm and start talking or we can always continue this pleasant conversation down at Southbury police station."

Both men laughed.

"On your way now lads as we have work to do." The Giant snarled as he picked up his mallet.

Kane took a step back with fear in his eyes. Getting something out of these two was going to prove extremely difficult. I stared them down for a minute and we then had a stroke of luck.

"What's going on boys?" A much younger man walked into the shop wearing the same style of grey boiler suit. He was very thin and had a mop of blonde hair. He was holding a chisel.

"Run Will," Shortie shouted. "Get the hell out of here."

Will stopped before turning on his heels and running back out the door.

Kane immediately gave chase but The Giant had lumbered towards me and grabbed hold of my shirt. I palmed a hand hard into his face but he did not budge. His face broke into a big smile as Shortie moved between me and the door.

"Don't give your friend much chance of catching the lad," The Giant laughed. "Also don't think you're going to walk out of here looking so pretty mister not-a-policeman."

"Very doubtful," Shortie agreed.

I made a face. "Would not be so sure of that."

In an instant I grabbed a nearby pot of paint and swung it with everything I had at The Giant's head. The pot was heavy and left my grasp immediately, glancing my foe on the side of the forehead. It was enough to send him reeling back with a cry of pain, releasing the hand that was holding my shirt. Before he could recover, I grabbed a second half –full pot and threw it with great accuracy straight at The Giant's nose. There was an explosion of blood as his nose splattered on impact. The big man fell backwards and crashed to the floor in a cloud of dust.

I turned to see Shortie looking on in a daze. Without a second thought I punched him on the jaw and sent him flying backward across a nearby counter. He laid spark out but The Giant was stirring, albeit groaning in pain. I decided to make my exit.

I turned as I got to the door. "Definitely not-a-policeman," I confirmed. "But still pretty."

It did not take me long to find Kane as he had apprehended the young lad called Will at the end of the short alleyway leading to Jill Smith's house. Kane was sat on top of the lad as he tried aimlessly to wriggle free. His efforts were in vain, getting weaker by the minute.

"I play a bit of rugger for the force, "Kane announced triumphantly. "Textbook tackle if I say so myself."

I smiled. "Let's see what Will has to say for himself."

Will swallowed hard. "I've done nothing wrong, let me go."

I studied him for a moment. "I really don't think you have done anything wrong Will, apart from taking a fancy to a very pretty nurse. But, and here's the thing, you might be able to help us find the person who killed that pretty nurse."

Will squinted, and then his eyes widened, "Jill was so nice and I would never have done anything to hurt her. She flirted and teased me but in my heart I knew she would never leave her posh fella for me."

I nodded for Kane to release his grip and Will slowly stood up, dusting himself down.

I walked forward and offered a cigarette, which Will gladly took. I lit it for him and one for myself, as Kane stepped back shaking his head.

Will looked up at me as he exhaled a large plume of smoke. "So how can I help?"
"Tell me about the times you met Jill, and in particular if you ever saw her with anyone?" I asked.

Will opened his mouth but thought for a moment and said nothing

I continued. "It doesn't matter if you were some lovesick puppy; we just want to find out what you might have seen."

Will closed his eyes for a moment. "I really did like her and the boys used to really tease me. They said she was old enough to be my mum. I would send her flowers and chocolates and she always knew they were from me. She always thanked me with a wink and a smile and told me I should find a girl of my own age. She said that the girl who would win my heart would win the world. It made me love her even more." He began to sob.

Kane shrugged and looked at me, slightly exasperated.

I smiled at Will. "You mentioned the posh fella. Do you know who he is?"

Will's eyes dropped to the floor. "No, but I got the feeling he was married or something. He was always quite cagey and never confronted me about my affectionate gifts for Jill. Is it him that you are after?"

I made a face. "No, but we do know who he is and yes he is married."

"Richard always said he was," Will mumbled.

"Who's Richard? One of your builder mates?" I asked.

Will laughed, "No the two blokes you were talking to earlier are Ox and Griff."

I instantly knew which one was Ox. "So, who is Richard?"

"The local postie," Will replied. "He's always around as you'd expect but the truth is I never saw anyone else hanging about."

I nodded. "Alright, but if you think of anything that might be of use, call into the station and ask for Constable Kane."

Will looked over his shoulder at Kane. "Does that mean we are done?"

"For now," Kane replied. "But don't go running off anywhere. We will find you."

Will nodded, still puffing on his cigarette. "Goodbye then," he muttered and then slowly ambled away before quickening his pace and then sprinting off."

Kane looked at me with a niggly off-centre smile. "Well, that was worth all the hassle Harry."

"Just a dumb love-struck lad," I confirmed. "Interesting that our friendly neighbourhood postman seemed to be egging the boy on though. Sounds like a bit of a gossip. Will be worth another chat at some point and see if he has any more information."

We strolled back to Kane's car, ready to head back to the station and re-think the next move. Kane was already incredibly nervous about updating McAldren before he had even put the key in the ignition.

8

We arrived back at Southbury Police station in good time. It felt strange voluntarily walking back into the place for the second time that day. McAldren was there to greet us by the door, sneering before we even spoke.

"A few dead ends I'm afraid sir," Kane announced confidently.

"Yeah, whatever." He dismissed the comment with a half-hearted swish of his hand. "Follow me."

Kane looked at me, puzzled, before following McAldren. I ambled behind.

McAldren led the way down to an interview room and paused with his hand on the handle. My first thought was that this would be another dubious suspect, just like the tramp from this morning.

"Our killer has become so confident that he is now playing games," McAldren stated before swinging open the door. I followed Kane into the room.

McAldren politely told a craggy looking sergeant that he could leave. The officer did as he was told, standing slowly and nodding whilst smiling at the man who was sat opposite him. "Reach out if you need me Jim," he said softly before leaving. Jim nodded in reply, mouthing the word 'thanks', before standing to greet the new arrivals.

Jim had a full head of silver hair and I aged him around early sixties. His face was badly pockmarked and there were large bags under his eyes. He was fairly stocky and wearing a very plain brown suit with a beige shirt and dark brown tie.

"This is Jim Johnson," McAldren announced. "Formerly Sergeant Johnson of Southbury Police, until he retired two years ago."

"You were just before my time sir but I have heard many tales about you from the boys," Kane held out a hand and briefly shook Johnson's hand.

"I'd already guessed you were former police," I announced as I stepped forward to also shake the man's hand. I swear he tried to crush my hand with such a hard squeeze.

McAldren cleared his throat. "And this is an amateur sleuth by the name of Harry Banner, supposedly assisting with this case.

Johnson did not look impressed. "How did you decide I was a former policeman?"

"Powers of deduction," I replied. "You have the same fashion sense as the Inspector here, and in fact most policemen I know."

McAldren ignored the comment and beckoned for Kane and me to pull up some chairs. McAldren did the same and sat alongside Johnson.

"Right Jim," McAldren said unusually softly. "Show the gentlemen what you've brought in"

Johnson nodded tentatively and then pushed a small brown envelope across the table. It was addressed to Jim Johnson at his home in Bale Street and had no stamp. The handwriting was extremely neat, like the old copperplate.

Kane picked up the envelope and slid out a Christmas card. The picture on the front was standard fare, a Christmas tree with wrapped presents at its base next to a roaring fire, with chestnuts on the grate. Kane opened the card to reveal the same style of handwriting as the neatly written address. All that was written was 'Number Four'.

We all shared a glance as the room fell silent.

"Is this in the same hand as the others?" I finally spoke.

McAldren nodded.

Johnson's face reddened in anger, "as soon as I received the card I knew it wasn't right. I just knew it had something to do with this bloody maniac in the papers. That's why I brought it in to the station."

I looked at McAldren. "Very odd though as until now all the cards have been delivered after a murder. Either our killer has got really confident and has decided to start playing games or…"

"….this is some stupid hoax." Kane finished the sentence.

Johnson shot Kane a challenging glare. "What are you insinuating lad?"

"Nothing against you sir," Kane stuttered apologetically.

"Although we can't rule out that some of your old colleagues might be having some fun with you." I quickly added.

Another death glare from Johnson. "Shows what little you know about the police lad."

I rolled my eyes. "We just have to be sure Jim or this could mess up the whole investigation."

McAldren made a face. "Believe me Banner, nobody in this station would have the nerve to pull such a stunt. They wouldn't know what hit them."

An uncomfortable pause followed.

I handled the card carefully, examining the handwriting once more. The words 'Number Four' written directly under a printed Merry Christmas declaration. So simple and yet so stark.

"Can I see the other cards?" I asked Kane.

Kane looked at McAldren, who nodded his consent.

Kane returned promptly with a folder containing the three Christmas cards cards found at the scene of each murder. I handled each card delicately. It was easy to confirm that each had been written in exactly the same way and that the handwriting in the fourth appeared identical to the first three. The cards were all made by the same company, Melville Cards. Each card has a different scene on the front but all were of a similar style.

"I assume no fingerprints?" I delicately held up the latest card.

"Your assumption is correct," McAldren replied indignantly.

"In that case, let's see if we can find any connection with Jim here and any of our previous victims." I smiled at Johnson.

Johnson visibly winced at the thought of me interviewing him.

McAldren cleared his throat. "I'll go and rustle up some tea."

As soon as the Inspector left the room I leaned forward and looked straight in Johnson's eye. "So Jim, obvious question, but have you ever met or had dealings with Lily Hutchins, Jill Smith or Peter Freeman?"

Johnson smiled. "Actually, yes."

I shifted in the chair. Not the answer I expected. "Who and when?"

"Freeman," Johnson replied quite smugly. "Of course, I have been keeping tabs on the case through what they report in the Southbury Echo. When I saw Freeman's face I just thought he looked familiar. It took some searching of the memory banks but then it came back to me."

"Did you arrest him?" Kane jumped in.

"No, not him," Johnson confirmed. "It was his crazy girlfriend. She stole a purse from a lady on a tram and Freeman came into collect her from the station after she'd been cautioned. This was just before I retired, about two years ago"

"Just a caution?" Kane continued.

"Yes, we could not prove the theft conclusively as the girl had got rid of the purse. Reckon she threw it in the river just before she was collared." Johnson was clearly still annoyed about the outcome.

I nodded. "What are your recollections of Freeman?"

Johnson made a face. "He seemed like a nice sensible young man who was very polite and apologetic for his girlfriend's behaviour. I just could not understand why he was with her. I think she had a screw loose or something. She kept laughing all the time and even stuck her tongue out at my young constable as he questioned her."

I turned to Kane. "Do you think this is the same ex-girlfriend who was killed in a road accident?"

"That's right." It was Johnson who answered. "She was hit by a tram. I saw it in the Echo last Christmas. Again, I recognised the picture, although it was taken when she was younger. She actually looked quite sweet but still with that crazy glint in her eye."

I sat back and tried to process the information. "It is tentative but at least we have something to go on. We just need to pull the police report on file for the girl and get in touch with the Echo. We need to build a picture of who this girl was and see if she had any connection with our other victims."

Kane nodded in agreement just as McAldren re-entered the room with a tray of steaming cups of tea. Kane filled the Inspector in on our conversation as he pushed the cups around the table, spilling a great deal of tea onto the table as he did so.

McAldren looked at me. "Where's your motive Banner? I mean Jim had nothing to do with this girl's death." McAldren looked at Johnson for reassurance. "I mean you didn't did you Jim?"

Johnson shook his head. McAldren looked back at me.

I arched an eyebrow. "Until we dig deeper, we will not know if this girl is the key"

McAldren glared me. "Probably just another dead end, just like all your other lines of enquiry today."

Kane went to speak but decided against it.

"Jim, did you notice anything when the card was delivered today?" McAldren asked Johnson.

Jim shook his head. "The card was delivered with the rest of the post. Nothing unusual at all."

"Maybe we should arrest the postman?" I arched the eyebrow again.

McAldren's face reddened. "At the moment he would be right up there with all your other leads Banner."

I said nothing.

"Kane, have Sergeant Lancet put a guard on Jim's home tonight" McAldren shouted as he headed out the door.

9

With thanks to Jim Johnson remembering the exact month and year that Peter Freeman's girlfriend was arrested, it did not take long for Kane to locate the file. We sat down together to review Johnson's report of the time.

The arrested girlfriend went by the name of Stephanie Walker. From the case notes it seemed pretty obvious that she had stolen the purse in that it was not the most subtle of thefts. The lady who had the purse stolen reported that Walker had approached her on the tram and exclaimed that there was a mouse near her foot. The lady had reacted with alarm, jumping backward as she looked to the floor. There was no mouse to be seen and Walker stated that she must have been mistaken and immediately left the tram as it came to a stop. The lady realised that her purse was missing from her bag and swore she saw Walker holding it as she stepped onto the pavement. The lady raised the alarm and a couple of male passengers chased after Walker, who had begun to run towards the river. She was eventually caught as she ran across the Longford Bridge by one of the male pursuers as the other raised the alarm with a nearby Bobby. The Policeman, a Constable Arkin, searched Walker but could not find the purse. He arrested her and she was questioned by Sergeant Jim Johnson.

Johnson's report described Walker's character as slipping between being logical and intelligent to moments of craziness boarding on insanity. Johnson concluded that Walker was playing a game but that it could not be proven that she had stolen the purse. It was noted that in all probability Walker had thrown the purse in the river once she had realised she would be caught.

A footnote mentioned that Walker was collected from the station by her boyfriend, Peter Freeman, who was of good character.

"There we have it," I said.

Kane made a face. "Maybe she had been arrested before?"

I shrugged. "Perhaps and worth a look. In the meantime I'll call the Echo and get them to retrieve the report of Stephanie Walker's death."

I made the call to the Editor at the Southbury Echo, who went by the name of Chris Nesbitt. The initial problem was that Nesbitt, a dour Irishman, knew me well and said, "I do not believe for one minute that Harry Banner is working with the police." It was only after I handed the receiver to McAldren to vouch for me that Nesbitt agreed to track down a copy of the paper. Unfortunately he was going to need time and so I was told to come to the Echo's office in the morning. Nesbitt did try and get McAldren to agree to some exclusive information on the Christmas Card Killer case in return. He got short thrift.

Kane returned with a few more slim looking files. He had been right in that Walker had been in trouble before. In fact she had been arrested three times over the course of five years prior to the incident on the tram. Twice for being drunk and disorderly and once for punching a taxi driver. On each occasion she was fined and it was recorded that the fine was settled by her boyfriend, Peter Freeman.

The final file was the report of Walker's death, which Kane had already previously read through shortly after Freeman's murder. Unfortunately it gave very little information and concluded that Walker's death was due to a tragic accident for which nobody was to blame. The tram driver, Colin Westwood, was reported to have been distraught and took early retirement shortly after the accident. His statement simply recalled that Walker seemed not to have been paying attention as she crossed the tramway. She had walked straight in front of his tram without warning and even though he had applied the brake sharply, it could not be helped that his vehicle hit Walker at some speed. She died at the scene.

Kane agreed to track down Colin Westwood's address, if he was still alive. Another lead that could wait until the next day as there was nothing more we could do that evening. I bade Kane a good night and headed for home.

I took the tram, which crossed the exact spot where Stephanie Walker was killed just over a year ago. I looked out of the window with a morbid fascination as to how the scene would have played out that day. The thought that crossed my mind was whether it really was just an accident. It was then I noticed something that prompted me to jump from the tram as it slowed.

Tied to a lamppost under a green Christmas wreath, almost next to the exact spot where Stephanie Walker had breathed her last, was a large bunch of red roses. People were rushing around minding their own business so it was easy to remove the flowers without being seen. If it had been nothing I would have subtly returned the flowers but I had a hunch and the hunch proved right.

Tucked inside the roses was a small white card with a handwritten inscription.

To my darling Stephanie
My life is so empty without you.
There will never by anyone else.
Sleep Tight my love
R

I read the card a couple of times before slipping it inside my jacket pocket. It would be good to check the handwriting next to the inscriptions in the Christmas cards left by our killer. I instinctively looked around, wondering if our potential killer was still nearby but there were a lot of people milling about, carrying Christmas shopping onto various trams and buses. Nobody stood out as inconspicuous.

I sniffed the flowers that were so fresh and beautifully cut. It was then I noticed the label on the small paper wrapping holding the stems together. The label read 'Kayley's'. I immediately headed for home with the roses in my hand.

Kayley's Florists was an establishment owned by Frank Kayley. Frank's shop was directly under my office, which was also where I lived. He was an amiable bloke who always looked out for me but he was also a crook. Frank was a member of The Firm and his shop was nothing more than a front for various illicit practices. The irony was that the answer to finding the Christmas Card Killer could well be on my own doorstep, coupled with the fact that Kayley very rarely actually sold any flowers.

When I arrived at Kayley's Florists a 'Closed' sign was showing at the entrance. I could see that some lights were on inside so tried the door but it was locked. I knocked twice with loud precise thumps to the door. As I waited I could not help but chuckle at Frank's rather delicate Christmas display in the window. A mock cardboard chimney complete with small hanging stockings and a painted log fire that really was a work of art. A set of teddy bears were placed in front of the fireplace in amongst various floral arrangements. I was so busy admiring the display that I had not noticed Frank Kayley walk up behind me until he tapped me on the shoulder.

"Looking for me Harry?" Kayley smiled, showing off his stained teeth.

I looked down at my squat pug-faced neighbour and smiled. "Hoping you can help me with a case Frank." I held up the bunch of roses without explanation.

Kayley frowned. "I'm curious. Come round the back."

I followed Kayley as he pushed open a tall wrought iron gate and then headed down a short and narrow alleyway that ran to the side of the shop. He beckoned me into his office at the rear of the shop. He told a couple of goons playing cards inside to "go and take a walk for a few minutes." The goons eyed me suspiciously as they pushed by. I did not recognise either man but Kayley's business was frequented by so many members of The Firm that being on first name terms with any of them was highly unlikely. This was coupled with the fact that I knew better than to stick my nose into Kayley's business and in return he left me alone.

The shop was the perfect front for The Firm. A very legitimate looking business with stacks of official forged books and records in the office should any ambitious Bobby come knocking. This was also highly unlikely given The Firm's paid-up associates in Southbury Police Force. I know that McAldren had wanted to bring Kayley down for years but there was not a senior officer who would support him. There had even been attempts to place a man on the inside but Kayley always sniffed them out before they even got in the door.

Kayley grabbed a bottle of single malt Scotch and poured two glasses. He handed me one without even asking if I wanted it. To refuse would be an insult and so I took the glass and drank. It was good Scotch.

Kayley raised his glass and smiled widely. He took a swig and then nodded towards the flowers. "What's the story then Harry?"

I raised an eyebrow. "I'm working a case and this very nice bunch of roses purchased from this very shop may hold the key."

"What's the case?" Kayley asked.

I had to be careful how I played this but there was no point in lying to Kayley. "I've been hired by the Mayor to track down the Christmas Card Killer."

Kayley squinted his beady, ferret eyes. "Well, that is a turn up for the books."

"I've even had to be nice to McAldren," I added.

Kayley feigned shock. "Now that I really don't believe."
I held up a hand. "I'll always level with you Frank."

Kayley rolled his eyes and spread his hands. "So, what does that fine bunch of flowers have to do with the Christmas Card Killer?"

"They were possibly bought by the killer himself," I replied whilst handing the flowers to Kayley.

Kayley made a face but said nothing

"They were left near to the place where a young woman was knocked over and killed by a tram last Christmas," I continued. "It is just a hunch at the moment but it may be that whoever is carrying out these killings is doing so because of the woman who was killed."

Kayley examined the flowers a little closer but kept silent.

"There was a card inside the flowers." I pulled it from my pocket and held it up for Kayley to read.

Kayley leaned forward. "All very interesting but here's the deal Harry...... I tell you what I recall but then you keep me and this shop out of your investigation. I do not need any kind of police attention on my business premises, no matter that I am a wholly innocent party."

I nodded. "You have my word Frank."

He grinned. "Good enough for me. Alright I do remember the spiv who bought this bunch. I sold them to him myself three days ago. I was waiting for a certain business associate to arrive when the spiv walked in."

I leaned closer. "So, you didn't just tell him the shop was shut and to get on his way, like you usually do."

Kayley stiffened. "Hardly got the chance. He immediately picked up this bunch marched over to the counter and plonked the money down on the counter. He had already turned on his heels before I could say a word. I just pocketed the money as the door shut behind him. A minute later my business associate arrived."

"Can you remember what he looked like?" I asked.

Kayley's eyes narrowed just slightly. "He wore a long black coat. He was very tall, over six and half foot I would say. He had a mop of black curly hair that had not seen a comb for a while and a poxy black moustache."

I nodded, "Anything else?"

Kayley thought for a moment. "That was about it but I do remember as he left that he had a very slight limp. I noticed it just as he opened the door. He seemed to pull up and wince a little."

"This is really helpful Frank." I said. "With your attention to detail you could come and work with me one day."

Kayley eyed me, looking me up and down. "I don't think so."

I tried not to grin. "Thanks for your help Frank and as promised I'll keep you out of this." I made for the door just as the two goons came back in.

I stopped as the goons walked past me and turned back to Kayley and smiled.

"Find him," Kayley snarled.

Within five minutes I was fixing myself another Scotch in my office above Kayley's shop. So much to ponder but the chase was definitely afoot. The thought that the killer may well have been literally yards away from where I lived sent a slight shiver down my spine.

I picked up the Lafayette and played *Winter Wonderland* before downing the Scotch and hitting the sack.

10

Despite all the theories running through my mind I slept well. I chose a grey pinstripe suit, white shirt and purple tie. A dark grey Fedora completed a smart, business like, appearance. More Stewart Grainger at Elstree than a backstreet Private Eye. I slipped on a thick black overcoat and walked out into the cold, dank, December morning. I headed off to the Hornet, parked at the back of Kayley's Florist shop and set off for the office of the Southbury Echo.

Chris Nesbitt hardly gave me a warm welcome but he offered me a chair in order to read a copy of the Echo left on a cluttered desk. The paper was dated as December 1st 1935, just over a year ago. The first murder by the Christmas Card Killer was on December 1st this year. Nesbitt had laid the paper down unopened but I quickly found the report of Stephanie Walker's death a few pages in. The photograph that accompanied the article showed a sweet looking young girl with black curly hair but just as Jim Johnson had commented, her wide eyes glared out from the page.

"Going to tell me what is in that article that is so important?" Nesbitt muttered.

I shrugged as I began to read. "One of many hunches we're looking at."

"Is she something to do with The Christmas Card Killer?" Nesbitt pressed.

"Just a hunch," I repeated.

"Not going to tell me anything, are you?" Nesbitt snarled

I hesitated before looking up and smiling. He took the hint and went back to his desk.

The report focussed on a young girl's life being tragically cut short, with the reporter concluding it was the result of an unfortunate accident. An elderly lady eyewitness concurred, stressing there was nothing the poor driver could have done. The driver was not named but it was reported that he was in a state of shock and unlikely to be back at work for some time. Stephanie Walker's father was quoted as saying that his heart was broken and it was cited that it was he who had provided the photograph for the Echo to use. The father was Paul Walker, a factory worker. There was no mention of the mother.

I made a note to find and hopefully speak to Paul Walker.

As I read each paragraph, I immediately re-read it to ensure that I did not miss anything significant. Nothing jumped out until the last line, which I only had to read once.

Miss Walker was tended to at the scene by district nurse, Jill Smith. Miss Smith happened to be in the vicinity at the time of the accident but her valiant efforts to save Miss Walker proved to be in vain.

"Bingo," I shouted. A connection to another victim of the Christmas Card Killer.

"Found something?" Nesbitt shouted over as he stiffened in his chair.

I turned and narrowed my eyes. "Might have another hunch but nothing concrete."

Nesbitt made a face but said nothing. I knew he was itching to have another read of the article and I'm sure he would have finally made the connection with Jill Smith. I closed the paper after carefully ripping out the article and made a swift exit, tipping my Fedora to Nesbitt as I went. Nesbitt grunted a goodbye and I'm sure he hardly missed a beat before grabbing the paper as the door shut behind me. I heard the scream of anger from the street below. I jumped back into the Hornet, tapped the ripped page secreted in my jacket pocket and set off for the police station with the wryest of smiles.

I headed south to the station but on arrival I did not even get a chance to put a foot in the building. Kane was waiting for me at the entrance.

"We've got to get to Jim Johnson's place as soon as possible," a flustered Kane spouted as we headed straight back to the Hornet. "McAldren is already there."

"Something happened?" I asked

He bit down on his lip for a moment. "Did not sound like good news."

I said nothing as Kane gave me directions to go south of the river, whilst acknowledging that I had "one stylish car."

I filled Kane in on my trip to the Echo and the confirmation of a connection between Jill Smith and Stephanie Walker.

Kane gave a shrill whistle. "So, if we find a link with Lily Hutchins then we can surely track down our killer. A grieving relative perhaps?"

I made a face. "The father was still kicking around a year ago so we should look him up."

"Will get onto it when we get back," Kane confirmed. "Also, when we are done at Johnson's, I have an address for the tram driver, Colin Westwood."

I nodded and took the prompt to tell Kane about the wreath left at the scene of Stephanie Walker's death, leaving out my conversation with Frank Kayley. Kane was still shaking his head and trying to make sense of it all as we arrived at Jim Johnson's house, marked by two police cars parked directly outside. Johnson lived in a turn-of-the-century grey brick terrace. Several neighbours had congregated on the pavement nearby, closely guarded by a policeman to stop them getting any closer to the house. Kane and I quickly got out of the car and I followed him straight into the house past another Bobby on the door, who yelled inside to announce our arrival.

"Through here," McAldren's voice barked from somewhere at the back of the house
McAldren was stood by the back door, looking out into the long garden. It was only when I was shoulder to shoulder with the Inspector that the grim reality was confirmed. A man's body lay on the ground right in front of where McAldren stood. I looked down on a dead Jim Johnson, his grey face contorted in a grotesque death mask. His throat had been slit with precision and yet his body had been positioned so neatly, with arms folded across his chest.

"This was placed in his hand," McAldren thrust a card towards me before I could say a word. I examined it and could see it was identical in every detail to the card that Johnson had bought into the station the previous day. The Christmas Card Killer had claimed their fourth victim.

I looked at McAldren for a few seconds. "I thought Johnson was being guarded?"

McAldren nodded. "That was the plan and if our killer had tried his luck at the front door then all would be fine. Seems he decided to clamber across several of the neighbour's gardens and break in round the back."

I feigned shock. "Quite the athlete!"

Kane was examining the door, which showed no sign of any damage. He turned and frowned, "so it looks like our killer somehow got Johnson to come outside. But how?"

I walked out into the garden to take a look. Johnson's garden was lined with high hedges on one side and a line of apple trees on the other. There was a small shed at the bottom of the garden at the end of a path. The garden was about 20 yards in length and it would have been relatively easy for someone to hide and observe the house. Did our killer simply wait and hope that Johnson would venture out? It was then I spotted the answer.

I knelt down and picked up a small pile of cigarette butts. "Looks like Johnson liked to come out for a regular puff." I showed McAldren and Kane the butts.

McAldren squinted his beady eyes. "So our man simply waited for Jim to pop out for a cigarette and then made his move."

Kane held up a hand. "Sorry but that would mean the killer was able to climb across several gardens and then secrete himself before being able to strike without Johnson even seeing him coming."

I closed my eyes to try and picture how it all happened.

"What are you thinking Banner?" McAldren prompted.

I reopened my eyes. "Military."

Kane stiffened. "That would make a lot of sense."

I looked for a reaction from McAldren but he said nothing.

Kane frowned. "We are up against somebody who is planning and executing every move with precision. He is always one step ahead of us. He probably crept in and watched Johnson's movements days before he actually struck"

McAldren's eyes narrowed. "He knows he can outsmart us and so now he's getting cocky too."

For a moment nobody spoke.

"Okay," I broke the silence. "He may have the upper hand at the moment but bit by bit we are learning more about the person we are looking for. It is somebody out to avenge the death of Stephanie Walker. Somebody who loved her so deeply that he is driven to kill anybody whoever crossed her. The ex-boyfriend who left her, the nurse who failed to save her life, the policeman who cautioned her."

McAldren just glared at me.

I continued. "We know that our killer was really close to Stephanie Walker in order to know who were all the people that supposedly failed her. We are most likely looking at a family member or maybe a new lover and we know this person undoubtedly has a military background."

McAldren cleared his throat. "Seeing as you know so much about the killer, I suggest you go and find him before he strikes again."

"We are going to track down Stephanie Walker's father sir," Kane confirmed. "He could hold the key to finding the killer."

McAldren scowled at Kane. "Well I suggest you get on with it whilst I go and try to explain this latest mess."
McAldren turned on his heels and stormed off.

About ten minutes later I drove Kane down to the nearest police phone box. Kane rang through to request that someone at the station track down an address for Stephanie Walker's father after providing all the details about her death and previous police cautions. Whilst the address was being sought it was time to go and pay the hapless tram driver a visit.

It took me a while to find Colin Westwood's house. It was in one of the poorer areas of Southbury, to the east. The estate, known as Parkheath, was pretty much a slum. Parkheath was just two long roads of grey terraced housing that converged on a wasteland covered in scrap metal and discarded furniture. Westwood lived at the end of Bampton Terrace, a stone's throw away from the wasteland. A few urchins were playing marbles in the gutter in the corner but quickly abandoned their game when they saw the Hornet draw up. The three kids came scurrying over to take a closer look.

I jumped out of the car and threw a shilling to each urchin. "If you watch my car whilst I'm in there," I pointed to Westwood's front door, "I will pay you the same again when I come out. Anybody comes near the car, knock loudly on the door."

"Alright mister, it's a deal." The lankiest lad confirmed.

Kane was shaking has head and smiling at my impromptu insurance policy as we walked up to Westwood's door. I ignored him and banged a fist twice on the door. We waited an age and I was about to knock again when the door finally creaked open.

Colin Westwood was the perfect portrait of a broken man. His thinning brown hair was uncombed and looked like it had not been washed for weeks. He looked gaunt with hollow eyes and a mix of grey and brown stubble lining his jaw and chin. His brown checked trousers hung below his waist, barely held up by a threadbare belt. His white shirt was covered in stains and he wore no shoes on his feet, just socks full of holes.

"Yes," Westwood almost whispered as he eyed me suspiciously.

"Colin Westwood?" Kane asked to confirm we had the right man.

"Who wants to know?" he replied, now turning his suspicious eye on Kane.

Kane held up a police badge. "We just need to ask you a few questions about the death of Stephanie Walker."

Westwood said nothing but just turned around and beckoned for us to follow him into the house. Kane led the way and I followed into a hallway that had a mixed aroma of damp, fried food and stale cigarettes. It was a smell that lingered in the lounge too as Westwood plonked himself down on a grey cloth armchair that had seen better days. He went to pick up a cigarette from a box on a coffee table by the side of the chair but cursed under his breath when he realised the box was empty. The ashtray was full of discarded butts. I instantly pulled out a packet of Woodbines and offered him a cigarette, which he gladly accepted with a grin. Kane declined the offer as I held the packet up, so I took one myself and lit it as Westwood did the same. I placed the packet on the coffee table as a gift and received another broad grin from Westwood.
Kane sat opposite Westwood on a rickety wooden chair, but I chose to remain standing.

Kane looked up at Westwood. "I'm sorry to bring up an event that must have been horrendous for you but anything you can recall could be vital in helping our investigation into a murder."

Westwood nodded tentatively. "I'm not sure how that young girl's death has anything to do with a murder."

"It could be that someone close to the young girl could be involved in a recent murder," I interrupted by keeping it vague. It might be that Westwood was earmarked as a future victim, so I did not want to alarm him. I could not help but think the killer would be doing him a favour.

Westwood thought for a few seconds. "Not the lunatic with the black moustache?"

I looked at Kane and then back to Westwood. "What made you say that?"

The colour seemed to drain from Westwood's face. "This lunatic was there that day. Moments after my tram hit the girl I climbed down from the cab, praying for a miracle and to find her alive and unscathed. I was in a daze but made my way over to the small crowd that had gathered. People looked at me with a mix of sympathy and concern and I even received a few gentle slaps on my back. Gestures of condolence I guess."

Kane sighed, "I can't imagine how horrible it must have been."

Westwood nodded as his eyes welled with emotion. "The scene has played in my mind every day and every night since."

I smiled knowingly, "take your time."

After a brief hesitation, Westwood continued. "As the crowd parted, I could see the body of the girl laid out on the floor. A nurse had been tending to her. She was not moving and a voice from the side confirmed she was dead. A gentleman had already placed his coat over the poor girl's body, covering her face. I stumbled forward and it was then out of nowhere that this lunatic went for me."

I narrowed my eyes. "How did he go for you?"

Westwood rubbed his chin vigorously, his hand shaking with nerves. "He came from the front of the small crowd, screaming that he was going to kill me. His eyes were full of rage and his fists were already raised. He tried to throw a punch and would heave surely taken my head off if a couple of by-passers had not intervened. They got hold of him and held him back as he continually screamed that I was a murderer. I just stood there, feeling totally numb as the lunatic raged how one day he would kill me and have his revenge."

I gave Westwood a curious look. "Apart from the moustache, anything else you remember about him?"

Westwood nodded. "He wore a long black coat and was very tall with black curly hair, but the thing that really stood out were his boots. I recall that they were so shiny; polished meticulously. I served in the army and I knew straight away they were military issue."

I glanced at Kane, who was taking notes. He looked up "What happened to the lunatic?"

Westwood made a face as he thought. "He managed to wriggle free and just turned on his heels and ran off into the night."

Kane glared. "Did you not tell the police this information at the time?"

Westwood almost smiled. "I did but the officer dismissed the incident. He told me not to worry about it and that this man was just some irate member of the public who had overreacted. The thing was I was so sure this man knew the poor girl I had killed."

I leaned forward. "And you haven't seen this man since?"

Westwood looked me square in the eye. "Not until last Tuesday."

I moved closer. "Last Tuesday?"

He went to speak, stopped and then gathered himself. "It was such a shock. I had just gone out to buy a paper and some ciggies from the newsagent a couple of roads away. I was walking in a daze as usual when I suddenly got a sharp jolt as someone glanced me shoulder to shoulder. He really connected and made me stumble sideways. I looked up and there he was, grinning at me. He was wearing the same long black coat but was also sporting a tatty old trilby hat."

"How could you be sure it was him?" Kane interjected

Westwood made a face. "He turned to me and lifted his hat, grinning like a Cheshire cat. He said that 'accidents can happen but you should be very careful'."

I glared. "So, he threatened you?"

He swallowed hard. "I guess so but I was too shocked to react. Before I knew it he had walked off down the road. I saw the same army issue shoes and I also noticed something else."

I shrugged but said nothing.

"I noticed he now had a limp," Westwood confirmed.

I stepped back and took a long draw on my cigarette. "You sure about that?"

Westwood stubbed out his own cigarette in the ashtray. "Very sure."

Kane gave me a puzzled look but I ignored him.

I nodded, "and no sign of him since?"

"None at all," Westwood replied.

"Did you not report this to the police?" Kane asked.

Westwood shrugged. "What would I have reported? The police did not want to know at the time so they were not going to be concerned about a pedestrian supposedly not looking where he was going."

"Tell me about the actual accident," I changed tact.

Westwood looked a little startled. "It was over in a flash," he said softly as his voice drifted off.

I nodded.

He continued after clearing his throat "One minute I was driving along, thinking about the end of the shift and going for a Christmas pint down The Crown. The next moment I look up to see this girl smiling from the side of the track and within an instant she just threw herself in front of the tram. Time seemed to slow down but it happened in a matter of seconds."

Westwood bowed his head and I could see his eyes were wet. I walked over and lit him another cigarette which he gladly accepted with a very shaky hand.

I stepped back and frowned. "The thing is Chris, the way you described the incident makes it clearly sound like the girl intended to kill herself. Are you saying she committed suicide?"

Westwood nodded and put the cigarette to his lips, inhaling sharply. "There was no doubt."

"Wait a minute," Kane put a hand on his head. "The police report concluded that this was a tragic accident. There was no mention of suicide."

Westwood smiled. "Initially I told the police exactly what I just told you. Then I got to meet the girl's father and he begged me to change the account. He wanted his girl to rest in peace and not be tainted by the fact that she had taken her own life becoming public. I agreed and told the police that I may have been wrong about the smiling girl throwing herself in front of the tram, even though I still see that smile every night as I try to sleep."

Kane shook his head.

I gave Kane the nod to say it was time to go and we made our excuses, as well as telling Westwood to call the station should he have any more sightings of the lunatic with the moustache.

After throwing a few more shillings to the urchins guarding the Hornet, we headed back to the station. After Westwood's revelation it was more important than ever to track down Stephanie Walker's father.

"Is there something you're not telling me Harry?" Kane asked with a sour face as I drove.

"What makes you say that?" I replied.

Kane tilted his head a little. "It was when Westwood described the lunatic with the moustache. It was like you already knew this character."

I turned for a moment and smiled. "Very perceptive Kane. It would explain why I lose so much at poker."

"Well?" Kane pressed.

I glanced across again. "I got a description of the person who left the wreath at the spot where Stephanie Walker was killed. I promised to keep the informant anonymous but their description is an exact match for Westwood's lunatic with a moustache."

11

We did not stay too long at the station. A very shapely female officer called Maggie made some tea and confirmed the address for Peter Walker, Stephanie's father. Kane re-opened the file on Stephanie Walker's death and I pulled out the report on the accident I had taken from the Echo's office. Kane grimaced at the thought of me ripping out the article without permission. I just smiled back and handed him the page to read.

Kane's eyes narrowed as he read. "This account is completely different to how Westwood described what happened."

"Uh huh." I nodded as I re-read the police report. "Same conclusion from your mob. Just an accident that was nobody's fault."

Kane made a face. "If Westwood is to be believed, then Peter Walker went to great lengths to make sure the memory of his daughter was not tarnished in any way."

We both drained the cups in unison as Maggie came in to collect the crockery. McAldren wandered in as well and pulled Kane aside for a private police discussion, making it clear that I was excluded. Perfect timing to slip Maggie one of my business cards after scribbling 'Call Me' on the back. She giggled and blushed but gave me a little sly nod before turning to go, nearly walking straight into the returning Kane.

Kane spread his arms. "Policewoman Middleton looked a little flustered. I trust you were a gentleman Harry?"

I held up a hand. "Always Kane, always."

I was still chuckling to myself as we got back in the Hornet

Peter Walker was listed as a retired fishmonger who lived south of the river. He lived alone, a widower of some twenty-two years. Stephanie Walker was twenty-seven when she died.

I took the main South Road.

"So, anything interesting from McAldren?" I asked

Kane squinted his eyes in the midday sun. "Just told me to keep a close eye on you and report everything we find. He heavily emphasised the everything."

I rummaged in the glove box and pulled out some black Oliver Goldsmith sunglasses. It was as I checked my reflection in the rear-view mirror that I noticed something. A red Morris Special directly behind me. There was just the driver in the car. He had a mop of blonde hair and wore a cravat. But it was the car that drew attention. It was a beautiful motor that I really liked the look of. The trouble was I had thought exactly the same when I saw the car behind me as I drove to the station after visiting Colin Westwood. Same driver same car, and I concluded no coincidence.

I cleared my throat. "Don't look round but we're being followed."

Kane looked totally bemused but resisted the urge to look. "Are you sure?"

I checked the mirror again. "As sure as I can be."

"Do you think it's Westwood's lunatic?" Kane spoke excitedly.

"Looks nothing like him," I confirmed.

Kane was silent, thinking.

"Alright, let's see who we are dealing with." I took a sharp left down a narrow road, inciting the sound of several horns from oncoming traffic.

The Morris did not have time to follow without smashing into the traffic. Kane grabbed his seat tightly with both hands, his knuckles turning white. He let out a yelp. I hit the accelerator and gunned the Hornet around a sharp bend and took a right turn onto another narrow road. Within seconds I was back at the junction to the South Road and shot back out into the main line of traffic. I then proceeded to overtake a couple of cars, bringing more feeble yelps from Kane. I then settled directly behind the red Morris.

"Good driving," Kane commented.

"Better than good," I corrected.

I could see the Morris driver moving uncomfortably in his seat as he gave me several glances through the rear-view mirror. He eased his foot on the accelerator and tried to put some distance between us. I simply matched his speed and kept on his tail.

"Don't do anything stupid," Kane whimpered.

The Morris suddenly veered to the right and gunned down the road to the harbour. The exact move I was expecting and I followed. As he checked his mirror, I was still very firmly on his tail. The next move I did not expect. The driver just slowed and pulled the Morris over to the side of the road. I pulled alongside, just in case he had any bright ideas of making another break for it.

I looked across and smiled. "I don't think I've had the pleasure."

The driver shook his blonde mop of hair and grimaced, "The name is Jake Power, I'm a Private Detective."

"Well Jake," I shouted back as a large lorry drove past, "who has hired you to follow me?"

Power held up a hand. "I genuinely do not know who the client is. Contact was through a phone call with instructions to leave a daily report with the landlord of The White Sails pub at seven o'clock this evening. An advanced payment was posted through my letterbox last night."

I shook my head. "You were hired without meeting the client. Bloody amateur. So, tell me, what was the brief?"

Power hesitated. "It was just to report your movements. The client wanted to know who you speak to and where you go. They seemed to know you pretty well. Told me where to pick up your tail this morning."

I rolled my eyes. "They obviously did not know much about you."

Power's eyes narrowed and he nervously adjusted his cravat. "What happens now?"

I leaned over the door. "Well Jake, you can deliver your report as intended this evening. You can even include our little chat."

Power looked a little puzzled. "So, you want me to carry on following you?"

"I don't think so Jake, do you?" I snapped.

No reaction.

"Look Jake," I continued. "Take the rest of the day off and deliver a report tonight. Leave everything else to me."
He nodded and smiled timidly before moving the Morris forward and slowly driving away, still checking his mirror as if unsure that I would follow.

Kane chuckled. "What the hell was that all about?"

I sat back, bemused. "I really have no idea but tonight we shall go for a pint at The White Sails and find out who is so interested in what we are doing."

Kane said nothing. I turned the Hornet around and drove back towards the South Road. "So, after the interlude, let's go and see Peter Walker."

Kane smiled. "As Private Detective's go, he wasn't in your league Harry."

I raised an eyebrow. "If you want a professional service, always hire Harry Banner."

Kane chuckled. "Yes, but in this case our mystery client could hardly hire you to follow yourself."

Thirty minutes later I pulled up outside Peter Walker's house. For a fishmonger, he had done really well. A quaint detached bungalow with a pristine green lawn to the front flanked by a long loose stone driveway. A grey Rover Coupe was on the driveway.

I had hardly put a foot on the drive when a deep voice bellowed out. "Can I help you gentlemen?"

A very tall man with a grey beard stood at the top of the drive, having marched straight out of the front door of the bungalow. He wore a dapper brown suit.

"Are you Peter Walker?" Kane called out

He stared off into the distance. "Who wants to know?"

Kane took a few steps forward and held up a badge. "I'm Constable Kane from Southbury station and this man is a Private Eye by the name of Harry Banner, who is currently assisting the force."

He looked us up and down. "Yes, I'm Peter Walker. You had best come in."

We followed Walker into the house and into a very neat and tidy front room. There was a chair by the window, with a newspaper and a pair of binoculars on the sill. No wonder Walker had spotted our arrival so quickly. Walker turned his chair around to face the room and sat down. He beckoned for us to take a seat on a couple of ornate wooden chairs.

Walker widened his eyes. "So, what do you want to see me about? Is it to do with our Stephanie?"

Kane nodded. "It is connected to the tragic death of your daughter and I apologise for having to re-visit what must have been a horrendous time for you."

Walker closed his eyes momentarily. "It was a year ago and I think about her every day. At least she is now at peace."

Without hesitation, I questioned, "at peace?"

He cupped his hands around his nose and mouth and then lowered them to his lap. "Stephanie had a lot of problems, just like her mother."

I made a face. "What became of her mother?"

Walker lowered his head. "She died when Stephanie was only five so I brought the girl up myself, with a lot of help from my sister."

I saw Kane look down to the floor.

I looked back at Walker and smiled thinly. "How did she die?"

He sighed. "Knocked over by a car, just two weeks before Christmas."

I nodded. "Did you witness the accident?"

Walker frowned. "No and it was not an accident."

Silence.

Walker looked up at me. "What is all this? Why the interest in Stephanie a year after she has passed?"

Kane turned both his palms up. "It is not so much about Stephanie but rather somebody who was close to her. Was she courting at the time of her death?"

He took a deep breath. "She had only ever courted one man and he was so good for her. I had never seen her so happy and content. His name was Peter Freeman and she met him at a stall he held on Southbury Market. For a short while I truly believed things would work out."

"You liked Peter Freeman?" I stated the obvious.

Walker actually grinned. "I did." He paused, "I read in the paper that Peter was murdered. Is this the reason for your visit?"
I shrugged. "In a way."

Silence.

I looked over at Walker and held his gaze. "You said that Stephanie had problems like her mother. Can I ask what sort of problems?"

Walker's eyes flicked down to the floor and then back to me. "Her mother was a depressive who had a lot of dark thoughts. She tried to kill herself on a couple of occasions before..."

"Before?" I repeated softly

Walker looked like a chill had gone down his spine. "Before she threw herself in front of a car and finally succeeded."

I nodded and went for my gentlest voice. "I'm so sorry." I paused, "was Stephanie a depressive too?"

Walker nodded. "She had all the same traits but the mood swings were so much more intense than I saw with her mother. Sometimes she would become violent and hit me and my sister. It all became too much when Peter left her and I made the decision to have her committed to Southbury Asylum."

Kane blanched. "How long was she there?"

Walker sighed. "Just a few months. She was a very different person when she was sent home. Very quiet and distant. Every day she would just get up and go out walking all day. When she came home, she would eat in silence and then go to bed. The same routine until the day she did not return."

I nodded. "The day she died."

"Correct," Walker looked straight at me.

I lifted my eyes to meet his. "We spoke to Colin Westwood this morning, the driver of the tram that knocked Stephanie over. He was adamant that your daughter walked in front of the tram on purpose and that he only reported differently after you pleaded with him."

Walker looked away for a moment. "It is true. I just did not want her to be remembered that way; the same way as her mother."

Kane hesitated before jumping in. "Are you absolutely sure that Stephanie was not meeting someone on her walks?"

Walker looked a little perplexed. "It is possible but she never mentioned anyone."

"Just one more question Mister Walker," I interjected. "Was Stephanie ever taught by a teacher called Lily Hutchins?"

Walker nodded. "My sister employed Miss Hutchins as a private tutor for Stephanie after she was expelled from school. Stephanie despised her and even attacked her. Miss Hutchins did not return."

"Uh-huh," was all I could muster in response.

Walker's eyes narrowed. "Miss Hutchins was also murdered, just like Peter. Both were killed by this Christmas Card killer. Are you saying that these murders are happening because of my Stephanie?"

"That's what we are trying to find out," I smiled as I stood to leave. "Preferably before the killer strikes again."

"If you think of anything that might help our investigation Mister Walker, please call the station and ask for Constable Kane." Kane managed a half smile as we made our exit. "Thank you for your time."

12

It took a while for one of us to find a voice as I drove Kane back to the station. We were both mulling over what Walker had said and trying to make sense of it all.

"Do you think Walker was playing us" Kane finally spoke as he glanced across his shoulder. "Could he be the killer?"

I shrugged. "If that's the case, he's a bloody good actor. Possible but I would happily wager that it's not him. Also, we know he's not Westwood's lunatic with the black moustache."

He shook his head. "Well now we know that Stephanie Walker is the key, so who the hell is this lunatic with the black moustache and how is acquainted with her?"

"We solve that and we solve the case," I stated the obvious.

No response but Instead Kane just looked out of the window.

As I pulled into Southbury police station I spotted Charlie Ransome arriving for his evening shift. Charlie was a desk sergeant and had been a good friend to my father. My father had also been a policeman, working with Charlie at Filton police station, which was some twenty miles north of Southbury. He was killed whilst foiling a bank robbery in Filton. His killer, and the gang of robbers, were never caught and brought to justice. Charlie was injured during the robbery and transferred to a desk job in Southbury to see out his career.

When not in the employ of Southbury police, I would get all my inside information from Charlie for a small contribution to his pension pot. I know that Charlie had spotted me as he had certainly been a passenger in the Hornet a few times, but he did not acknowledge and neither did I. To safeguard our arrangement it was for the best.

Kane gave me a weary glance as he opened the passenger door. "So now it seems our only lead is this bloke who hired the Private Detective, Jake Power. Or should I say Private Defective?"

I nodded. "Very good Kane, you should be on the stage. You'd give George Formby a run for his money."

Kane sighed.

"Anyway," I continued, "If my theory is right then I think we'll find that Power's client is nothing but a red herring. I'll pick you up from here at six-thirty so we can get to The White Sails in good time."

Kane now scowled. "I'd better go and fill McAldren in."

"If you would," I grinned.

Kane grunted and trudged towards the station entrance, muttering under his breath. "So now who's the comedian?"

As I drove back through Southbury on the way back to the office, it really struck me how much the town was gearing up for Christmas. Bright shop window displays and a strong aroma of mulled wine and chestnuts in the air. Christmas Day was still a week or so away and yet you would think it was tomorrow. The need for some Christmas spirit now seemed to start earlier each year but this year for the residents of Southbury it was mixed with fear and trepidation. Until the Christmas Card killer was caught, nobody would sleep easy. Truth was that unless someone had a connection with the deceased Stephanie Walker, they had nothing to fear.

I parked the Hornet down a side road next to Kaley's shop. Even Frank's window display was suddenly heavy on holly and bright read berries.

"Southbury Echo," the street corner seller shouted with his usual strained voice. "Read all about it. Christmas card killer strikes again. Victim number four."

I walked across the road and bought a copy of the Echo. The seller only had a few left; the Christmas Card Killer had undoubtedly been good for trade.

I read the front page as I walked.

Fourth Victim for the Christmas Card Killer

Southbury's very own Jack the Ripper has struck again. The body of a retired Southbury Police Sergeant, Jim Johnson, was discovered this morning at his home. His throat had been slit and the now familiar Christmas Card placed on top of his body. It seems that Mr Johnson was another unfortunate random victim of the deranged killer who has left the whole town living in fear at a time when we should all be looking forward to the festive celebrations of the Yuletide.

Evidently the Police are no nearer to finding the killer and there have even been unconfirmed reports that the force has taken to hiring a Private Detective to solve the case for them.

Inspector McAldren of Southbury Police told the Southbury Echo, 'We are asking all Southbury Residents to be vigilant in helping to catch this fiend, whether they be a Butcher, Baker or Private Detective.'

Chris Nesbitt did not get much change out of McAldren but he could not resist commenting on my new role, without naming names. I was the most high profile, and obviously the best, Private Detective in Southbury. A lot of people would have figured it out.

As I walked into the office I threw the copy of the Echo down on my cluttered desk. I really did need to get down to some paperwork when this case was done and dusted. I poured myself a single malt and let the bite of the fermented barley sit in my throat. My shoulders were tight with tension. I closed my eyes and took another dram. I walked to the window and looked out into the late afternoon dusk. Some candles twinkled from a window across the street and caught my eye. Somewhere out there the killer was plotting his next victim and writing a Christmas Card like no other. No thoughts of joy to the world but rather a notice of pending execution. For a moment I doubted myself. What if I did not find the killer?

I drained the Scotch and picked up my trusted Lafayette. I instantly played *Silent Night* and felt the tension begin to lift. All doubt was gone. The reputation of Harry Banner was on the line like never before but I resolved there and then that I would track down the killer if it was the last thing I ever did.

13

Before leaving to pick up Kane I changed into a clean black suit, white shirt and red tie. The red was for a touch of Christmas and far from inconspicuous but was soon covered with a long black overcoat. After selecting a matching black Fedora, I headed out into the darkness of early evening.

Kane was waiting outside the station as I pulled up in the Hornet. He climbed straight into the car without a prompt, seemingly grateful that I had put the roof up on a cold December night. I drove off straight away.

"I assume McAldren was in good spirits when you reported on our progress?" I asked without hiding the sarcasm

His face shut down. "McAldren would only have been happy if we'd actually brought the killer in. Even then he would find fault somehow."

"His quote in the Echo did smack of desperation," I chuckled.

"Uh-huh," Kane was deep in thought.

I arched an eyebrow. "So did McAldren have any theories based on our interviews with Colin Westwood & Peter Walker?"

Kane made a face. "He initially wanted to bring Peter Walker in. Had him down as prime suspect number one until I managed to dissuade him."

"I wouldn't completely dismiss him as a suspect but unlikely." I looked across, "more likely if Walker is involved that he got someone else to do it."

Kane shrugged, unconvinced. "Possible."

"What did McAldren think about our run-in with the intrepid Jake Power?" I asked.

Kane frowned. "He hates all Private Eyes as you know so hearing about Power did nothing to lighten his mood."

I made a fake mortified face.

Kane sighed loudly. "McAldren's parting shot was to say that you might as well have arrested the postman after all."

A few minutes later we arrived at The White Sails pub. I pulled up across the road.

I turned to Kane. "This is how we are going to play it. You go into the pub and order a beer. Then take a seat by the window where you can see the Hornet and I can clearly see you. Once Power hands over the report, hold up your hand above your head. I'll then make my way in to collar our mystery man."

"Right," Kane nodded. "But would it not be easier for us both to go straight in?"

"It would," I agreed. "However our mystery man knows who I am and if he spots me in the pub then that would be that."

"Understood," Kane nodded again.

Kane climbed out of the Hornet into the chill of the night and walked over to the pub. Five minutes later he was sat by a window in clear view. I sat patiently and watched. Finally, after about ten minutes, Jake Power came shuffling down the road. He looked hesitant and nervous, looking over his shoulder at every opportunity. Power then caught sight of the Hornet and stopped for a moment. Thankfully he did not wave but instead entered the pub with a folder clearly tucked under his arm. His fake report.

Power came out of the pub a few minutes later and hurried away, this time without a second glance. I got out of the car and stood by it. My eyes were now set firmly on Kane. Within seconds the hand went up and I ran across the road. Kane was already stood at the bar as I entered and signalled that the file had been taken to a back room. Without hesitation I charged behind the bar with Kane in pursuit, despite the protestations of a buxom barmaid. Kane held up his police badge to shut her up.

I could hear voices from a small stockroom directly behind the bar and immediately barged in. There were two men in the room perusing the blank fake report from Power. One I assumed was the landlord and the other I had last seen this very morning. It was Chris Nesbitt, editor of the Southbury Echo.

I slowly shook my head. "A very underhand way to get a scoop Nesbitt, but then why am I not surprised. Hacks like you would sell their own mother to get a good exclusive."

Nesbitt pointed at me. "Don't play the innocent with me Banner. You'll go to any length to crack a case and I'm no different."

"The difference is I'm going to charge you with wasting police time," Kane almost snarled the words.

"That's not going to happen," Nesbitt announced with confidence. "Not unless you want me to press charges against Banner for vandalising the newspaper I allowed him to see this morning."

I put a hand on Kane's shoulder. "Best let it go."

Kane did not look happy. "Just stay out of our way Nesbitt or I'll recommend to Inspector McAldren that he only speaks to the Southbury Journal from now on."

Nesbitt sneered. "Only if you want nobody to know about what's going on. You need our readers more than we need anything from you. It will be a tip off from the public that will nail this fiend."

I said nothing as I knew Nesbitt was right. I tapped Kane's shoulder again to signal it was time to go.

"So, what can you give me?" Nesbitt shouted as we made for the door. "Or shall I just use my imagination and write about the thick plod working with a blundering PI and getting nowhere fast in solving this case?"

I turned and looked back. "Blackmail too! You really are something Nesbitt."

Nesbitt smirked as if I'd given him a compliment.

"Print what fairy tale you like, just as you normally do." I left the room and caught up with Kane who was waiting in the lounge bar.

"That man is due a comeuppance," Kane seethed.

I just nodded.

We went to leave the pub but stopped short after being hailed by one of the customers.

"Good evening Gentlemen," was the friendly greeting from the bloke sat at the bar cradling a half-pint of mild.

I recognised the postman we had met outside of Jill Smith's house the day before. The distinct black curly hair and moustache was the giveaway.

"Hi," I held out a hand, "Jones wasn't it?"

"Yes, Richard Jones," he shook my hand and nodded to acknowledge Kane. "How's the investigation going? Will I be reading about Lord McNair's arrest in the echo tomorrow?"

With impeccable timing, he muttered the words just as Nesbitt walked though the pub.

"What's this about Lord McNair?" Nesbitt stopped in his tracks

"A dead-end Nesbitt," I pushed him away. "Nothing for your sleazy rag."

Nesbitt reluctantly left the pub without another word, almost barging Kane out of the way.

Kane stepped up to the bar "Be careful as when we're gone, he'll circle back and try and get a story out of you."

Jones nodded and reached for his beer.

Kane looked up at me. "Well, you reckoned it was the postman Harry. He even fits the description of Westwood's mystery lunatic. Shall we arrest him then?"

"Arrest me?" Jones suddenly looked really nervous, just like when we met him before.

I laughed. "You're safe."

Jones exhaled loudly and downed the rest of his beer. "Can I get you a drink?"

Kane replied. "Thanks but we must be going."

"No problem," Jones smiled broadly. "Although I'm glad I bumped into you as something unusual happened yesterday and it might be something or nothing."

Kane looked up. "What was it?"

Jones signalled to the barmaid for another beer

"I'll get this," I held up a pound note.

"Very kind of you," Jones grinned cheekily.

"So, what happened?" Kane snarled impatiently.

Jones hesitated and looked unsure. "The thing was I was doing my round on Bale Street when I was approached by a gentleman who asked if I would be so kind as to deliver a Christmas card for him as he did not want to be seen by the person he was sending it to."

"What did this man look like?" Kane asked

"He was very tall and had this horrible grey beard," Jones confirmed

I half-smiled. "Did you deliver it for him?"

Jones shook his head. "No, I told the cheeky bugger to buy a stamp like everyone else."

"Interesting," I looked over at Kane.

"Like I say probably nothing," Jones was a handed his beer by the barmaid and instantly took a gulp. The barmaid took my note and returned promptly with change

"Thanks for the information Richard but as you say probably nothing," I looked over at Kane and nodded towards the door. Time to go.

Once we were out on the street, Kane stopped dead and glared at me. "Jim Johnson lived on Bale Street and received a card through the post yesterday, without a stamp"

I nodded. "Also, the man who Jones just described fits the description of Paul Walker to a tee."

14

I woke the next morning with a constant niggle. The feeling I was missing something that could seemingly be glaring me in the face. Something that would solve the puzzle of the Christmas Card Killer and spare the next unfortunate victim.

Kane had committed to bring Paul Walker into the station for questioning but I just could not see him as the killer. Call it an instinct, although I truly hoped I was wrong. But then what would he say about being identified as the man behind the delivery of the Christmas card to Jim Johnson? Perhaps he was in cahoots with another but then who?

Another instinct told me that the killer was mercifully nearing the end of his list of victims. There could not be many more out there who had wronged Stephanie Walker. On one hand at least the spree may soon be over but then the trail may go cold and the case never solved.

There was a real winter chill in the morning air as I stepped outside. I raised the lapels of my blue overcoat and tipped my Fedora to offer some shelter from the wind. I hurried past Kayley's Florist shop with a brief nod to Frank as he stood in the window re-arranging his Christmas display. Frank loved to keep up the pretence of being a legitimate businessman.

I drove the Hornet down to the station in what was starting to become a routine. It was like I had proper job. A regular Bobby.

It was ten o'clock when I arrived and Kane confirmed that Walker was in custody, waiting to be interviewed. Kane took me to his desk after arranging for some tea to be brought down. We had barely sat down when McAldren appeared and plonked his backside down on the side of Kane's desk.

Straight away McAldren made a face. "So, do we have our man?"

I shrugged. "Possibly, but then again maybe not."

Not what the Inspector wanted to hear. "Well, it all seems to fit as far as I can see. What I can't understand is why you didn't crack it sooner Banner and in the end you just happen to get lucky by bumping into a stranger in a pub. What a detective you are!"

Another shrug. "If it's him then I'll take that on the chin but let's wait and see."

"We're all hoping we've got our man," Kane added.

McAldren's leg began to twitch. "Can I trust you clowns to get this right or do you want me to take the interview and show you how we get a confession the McAldren way?"

I frowned. "Thanks for the offer Inspector but we've got it covered."

McAldren folded his arms tightly to his chest and looked me in the eye, and then turned to glare at Kane. He huffed and left without another word.

It was fair to say that Paul Walker looked bewildered as he sat with his lawyer. I gave him a friendly smile and sat down next to Kane. Walker and his lawyer sat on one side of the desk whilst Kane and I sat facing them from the other side. A young constable sat nearby with a notepad.

The lawyer, a very dapper gentleman with a handlebar moustache, introduced himself as Jason Kilman. He then immediately frowned. "What on earth is your intention of bringing this fine upstanding man into your station today?"

Kane's eyes narrowed. "We would like to ask Mister Walker about an incident that has been reported that may be significant in catching the man dubbed the Christmas Card Killer by the press."

Kilman gave a disapproving scowl. "Well spit it out sir, whatever is this incident you speak of?"

Kane focussed his attention on Walker. "Can you confirm if you have ever met a former Sergeant of Southbury Police by the name of Jim Johnson?"

Walker nodded tentatively. "I met him a couple of years ago by chance. I was in a pub with my daughter and her then boyfriend, Peter. My daughter, Stephanie, had recently been cautioned by Sergeant Johnson over a trivial misunderstanding concerning a missing purse. Then lo and behold the Sergeant came into the pub with a couple of his police colleagues."

Kane raised an eyebrow. "Did something happen?"

Walker gave a half-nod. "Stephanie was quite upset when she saw Johnson but Peter calmed her down and told her to pretend he was not there. However, Johnson had other ideas and as the night drew on he became more boisterous with his pals as the drink took over. He inevitably spotted Stephanie and began to loudly goad her, warning others in the pub to hide their valuables as there was a thief about."

"What did you do?" Kane pressed.

Walker made a face. "We actually got up to leave on Peter's insistence. However, as we neared the door, Johnson stepped across my path and asked who I was. When I confirmed I was Stephanie's father, he began to insult her and called her all kind of names. Stephanie ran out of the pub in tears."

I grimaced. "What happened?"

Walker was hesitant but finally admitted, "I punched him."

I nodded. "Did you hit him well?"

Walker's eyes widened. "Knocked him out but I did not hang around and left the place sharpish."

I arched an eyebrow and leaned closer. "Did you ever see Johnson again?"

Walker blinked, looked at his lawyer and then back to me. "No, although I did expect to be arrested over the following days but it did not happen. Johnson must have decided to let it drop."

"And have you had reason to see Jim Johnson since that day?" Kane asked.

Walker shrugged. "No, I had not given him another thought until I saw his picture in the Echo. Another victim of this Christmas Card Killer that we talked about yesterday. I suppose it is another victim connected to Stephanie but just because I once punched him does not mean I would now want to see him dead. And why would I want to kill Peter or Lily Hutchins?"

I tilted my head a little and smiled. "You see Peter we could not decide yesterday whether you were completely innocent or actually a great actor. My hunch was innocent but then we came upon a witness last night who described an incident that suggested maybe I was wrong."

Kilman held up a hand. "Who is this witness?"

Kane sat upright. "A concerned member of the public who reported seeing a man matching Mister Walker's description loitering near the house where Jim Johnson lived two days ago. By the next day Jim Johnson was dead,"

Kilman leaned back. "Is that all you have? Somebody who may have passed a resemblance to Mister Walker was seen walking down a road."

Paul Walker went quite pale.

Kane leaned forward. "It was a bit more than that. The witness described how this man asked him to deliver a card to Jim Johnson's house. A Christmas card."

Kilman smiled. "Where was this sighting exactly?"

"Bale Street," Kane confirmed.

Kilman looked across to Walker, "have you ever been to Bale Street?"

Walker nodded very tentatively. "I was there two days ago. I received a card in the post asking me to attend a house on Bale Street on that very day. I was told to bring the card with me and that I would be in line to receive notice of an inheritance from a distant relative."

I arched an eyebrow. "What was the number of the house?"

Walker thought for a moment. "Number twenty-two."

A small grin played on Kane's lips. "The address of Jim Johnson, who you earlier admitted to attacking in a rage."

Walker shook his head. "I did not know it was Johnson's house and besides there was nobody there when I called."

"Do you still have this invitation that was sent to you?" I asked.

Walker paused, his mind flashing back. "No, I gave it to a postman who ripped it up."

I lifted my hand to my chin. "What made you give it to the postman?"

Walker shrugged. "As I walked down the path, the postman came in through the gate. He thought I might be the person who lived there but I explained about the bizarre invite. He took the card from me and said I'd been lucky as it was an obvious con. He then ripped the card up and wished me a good day."

Kane dived right in. "What a very convenient story. Maybe you are that brilliant actor after all."

Walker started shaking. "It is the truth I tell you. I had nothing to do with the murder of Jim Johnson or any of the other victims. I am not the Christmas Card Killer."

Kilman did his blustering best to order Kane to release his client due to a lack of concrete evidence but Kane insisted Walker was taken to a cell whilst further investigations were conducted. The lawyer went so red with rage that I feared he would have a heart attack. Walker sat in total silence, in a state of complete shock.

Walker was led away, Kilman was escorted from the station and Kane headed off to update McAldren. I stayed in the empty interview room, lit a cigarette and pondered the situation. Something did not smell right here and it was not the cheap tobacco.

Kane was gone for about twenty minutes but on his return he came bursting into the room, looking extremely flustered. He was holding a piece of paper in his hand.

"The front desk just took a call with an urgent message for you Harry," Kane threw the note down on the table.

I lit up another cigarette and quickly read the message. It was from Maria Donatella, principal Burlesque dancer at The Blue Bay club. I still worked at the club occasionally, playing trumpet in the Big Band. I had not been in for a few weeks. The note stated that I was to meet Maria urgently at The Blue Bay but must come alone. It was a matter of life and death concerning the Christmas Card Killer.

Kane leaned forward with his hands on the table. "Maria Donatella is the girlfriend of the notorious crook Maxwell Smooth Gray. What's this to do with Harry? Why is she looking for you?"

"Difficult to say," I answered wryly. "I play trumpet at The Blue Bay now and again and know Maria well."

Kane nodded towards the note. "What could she know about the killer? Do you think it might be Smooth?"

I smirked. "Not really Smooth's style. He's not known for any kind of subtlety when it comes to using violence."

I stood and spread my hands. "I best go and find out what this is all about."

The truth was I was as puzzled and intrigued as Kane. I promised that I would come straight back to the station as soon as I had spoken to Maria but in return asked Kane not to tell McAldren where I had gone. A few minutes later I was in the Hornet and heading for The Blue Bay.

Maria met me at the main entrance to the club and ushered me nervously inside. She looked stunning in a black leotard and black tights. Her long black hair was tied back showing off her stunningly beautiful face; a flawless complexion with those big dark Italian eyes. She tried to direct me to a side room but we both stopped dead as Smooth appeared, puffing on a large Cuban cigar. Two goons appeared and flanked him. Smooth just stood there, staring at me. He was a tall threatening figure. He was wearing a dark blue pinstripe trousers held up by navy braces stretched over a dress white shirt. The sleeves of the shirt were rolled up and the collar loosened, without a tie.

Smooth just stood there studying me.

I broke the silent tension. "Anybody care to tell me what is going on?"

He gave me a look and then spoke directly to Maria. "What did I say I did not want you to do?"

I looked at her, waiting for an explanation.

She was shaking her head, looking tearful. "You said not to involve the police Smooth and I didn't. We can trust Harry."

He frowned. "I said I would take care of it. We don't need Banner."

I let loose a deep breath. "Can someone at least fill me in on what has happened?"

"Please Smooth," Maria pleaded.

Smooth hesitated but finally relented. "In my office."

Maria and I followed Smooth up the stairs and into his office. His two goons stood outside guarding the door, I could not resist patting one of the brutes on the shoulder as I walked by. His name was Marcus, a six-foot muscle head with no sense of humour who just happened to detest me.

Smooth took a seat at his desk, still puffing on his cigar. Maria looked up at me, her big eyes widened but were full of fear. With a shaking hand she took out an envelope and handed it to me. It was simply addressed to *Maria Donatella c/o The Blue Bay Club.* I opened the envelope and pulled out a Christmas Card. I opened the card and read the inscription:

'Last is Number Five' written directly under a printed Merry Christmas declaration.

For a moment I just stared at the message; the same unmistakable handwriting I had seen in the card handed to me by Jim Johnson. Finally I looked up. First at Smooth still puffing on his cigar and then to Maria, gawping with wide eyes.

I still considered for a moment. "When did this arrive?"

"This morning," Maria replied. "In the first post."

Smooth huffed. "Just some crank and if he tries anything, well….let him try."

I sighed. "Thing is this follows the same pattern of the last victim of the so-called Christmas Card Killer. A card was sent to him before he was murdered. The killer is now playing games. Previously he only left a card once the victim was dead"

"I told you it was serious Smooth," Maria blurted.
"Oh I forgot, Banner is working for the police these days." Smooth smirked.

"Hired to work with them, not for them," I replied.

Maria ignored both comments. "Why me Harry?"

"First of all," I said, "did you ever know a girl by the name of Stephanie Walker?"

Maria shook her head, puzzled. "I don't think so. The name does not ring any bells."

Smooth looked at me hard. "Why the question Banner?"

I flashed a frown back at him. "All the victims of this killer are linked by an association with a girl called Stephanie Walker. In the eyes of the killer, all had wronged her somehow."

Smooth pointed at me with his cigar. "Where is this girl now?"

"Dead," I replied. "She died last Christmas when she was hit by a tram. It now looks like it was suicide."

"Any relatives?" Smooth went back to puffing on his cigar.

I nodded. "Her father, and the police currently have him in custody as prime suspect number one,"

"Case solved then," Smooth leaned back in his chair.

I just frowned and said nothing.

"You don't think he's the killer do you Harry?" Maria pressed,

I shook my head.

"So, what do I do?" Maria was on the verge of tears.

"First we need to work out your connection with Stephanie Walker," I replied. "Do you think she could have worked at The Blue Bay?"

Maria swallowed hard. "We have all employees logged in a set of ledgers."

Smooth sniggered.

Maria gave him a filthy look. "Thanks to me The Blue Bay is run as a legitimate business."

Maria led me away to another office. Smooth and his goons followed behind at a slow amble. This office was really small and pokey and full of paperwork. Smooth and his goons stayed outside as Maria began flicking through a large red leather-bound book as I stood by the door. She had just about finished going through the first, and most recent, volume when Maria suddenly stopped. She held the book up and looked closer at a particular handwritten entry. Finally she handed me the ledger, her finger pressed on the entry.

Stephanie Walker. Dancer. Lacks experience but sure to catch the eye of every gentleman. Started 9th September 1935. Dismissed 21st September because of tendency to violence.

I felt a chill. "Do you remember her now?"

Maria spun towards Smooth. "It was that really strange girl. One minute she was all sweetness and like and the next she was attacking one of the other girls, scratching and biting."

Smooth nodded.

Maria turned back to me. "I fired her Harry on the third occasion she attacked one of the girls, pulling her hair. At first she was very repentant and apologetic but when I refused to change my mind, she went for me too. I had to slap her so hard and she fled in tears. Everyone called her Step, that's why the name did not register."

I made a face. "We have a problem."

Smooth's eyes narrowed. "Banner, do you seriously think this killer has any chance of laying a finger on Maria with me around?"

I smiled. "I'd like to think not Smooth but indications are that this bloke is ex-army and he has already evaded a police guard to kill one of his victims."

Maria looked me straight in the eye. "What do you recommend Harry?"

"Go into police protection," I suggested.

Smooth was not happy. "That is not going to happen Banner, I'm not having any Rozzers sniffing round here. And besides did you not just say that he found his way around a police guard?"

He had a point. "Then you're going to have to guard Maria at all times and with a heavy guard. She must never be left alone."

Smooth nodded slowly. "That I can manage but I don't want a word of this to your new friends in blue Banner. If you do then I'm sure Marcus here would be glad to break every bone in your body."

Maria glared at Smooth as Marcus shuffled slightly, smirking at the thought of giving me a beating.

I shrugged. "I'd best go and find this killer then."

Smooth did not respond but just took a big puff on his cigar. I made my exit, almost going shoulder to shoulder with Marcus as I pushed my way of the door. Maria followed me and grabbed my sleeve just as I reached the lobby. Marcus and his fellow goon stood just behind her like a couple of guard dogs, which I was actually pleased to see.

Maria glanced back at her guards, and then waited a beat. She pulled my sleeve again and edged me to the side by a large Christmas tree. "I'll be alright Harry. Smooth will make sure I'm protected but please find this man."

I shrugged. "Trust me."

15

As I drove back to Southbury police station, those final words rang in my ears. What if I got this wrong and Smooth could not protect Maria? Failure was just not an option.

I had only just climbed out of the Hornet when Kane came out to greet me. "What did you find out at The Blue Bay Harry?"

I was going to have to play this carefully. If I told Kane the truth then he would be obliged to call it in. "Just a red herring. Maria was paranoid she was going to be the next victim as some drunk keeps following her around. Nothing in it."

Kane shook his head. "Waste of time then?" I was not sure he totally bought it.

I shrugged.

Kane made a face. "McAldren has been giving Walker the third degree, looking to scare a confession out of him. All to no avail but he did repeat that Stephanie Walker spent time in Southbury Asylum for a few months before her death."

I thought about that for a moment. "We should take a drive out there."

Kane went back into the station to square it with McAldren and then returned promptly to join me in the Hornet.

I stayed pretty quiet on the drive to Southbury Asylum, which was situated around ten miles north of Southbury. Kane is an astute man and I am sure he wanted to press me further about Maria, but he wisely kept schtum. The asylum was set in large grounds of around five hundred acres. Once through the main estate gates it was still a trek down to the main building, which was a horrible gloomy grey Victorian infirmary.

We were met by a nurse, a matron I think, at the main entrance. She was a large lady with a glum officious face and I certainly would not have messed with her. The place was eerie and I felt a shiver run down my spine as a shrill scream echoed down the corridor. Matron did not even flinch.

Kane explained why we were here and showed his police badge. Matron studied it for what seemed like an age and then finally led the way to a small waiting room. She announced she would return presently with a doctor. We were not offered any refreshments.

After about fifteen minutes the waiting room door swung open and a man walked in wearing a long white coat. He was aged around sixty with tufts of wiry uncombed grey hair circling his bald crown from ear to ear. He wore glasses that sat on the tip of his nose, and both nostrils were full of grey hair.

He looked down his glasses to observe us both. "My name is Doctor Underhill, how can I help you?"

Kane rose a little from his seat. "We are here to talk about a former patient at the asylum. Her name was Stephanie Walker."

Underhill frowned and then took a seat opposite. "I remember Miss Walker well. Such a tragedy that she died so young."

I sat forward. "What do you remember of her whilst she was under your care?"

Underhill sat back with his hands locked behind his neck and his elbows sticking out. "She was a schizophrenic. Her dominant character was very normal and very lovely but sadly the devil voices in her head would not let her be normal all the time."

I nodded. "When Stephanie came to you I am assuming the voices had become dominant but who made the decision for her to be committed?"

Underhill stared at me. "It was in fact the girl herself. She was brought here by her father, who did not seem too pleased at his daughter's choice."

Kane dived right in. "Did the father make any threats to you or anyone in the hospital?"

Underhill turned and stared at Kane now. "I cannot say he did."

Kane sat back a little deflated.

Underhill held out his arms with palms upwards. "Why the interest in this girl as she has been dead for over a year?"

Kane explained. "We have information that someone who was close to Miss Walker is now seeking revenge on anyone who wronged her. It is as if they blame them all for Miss Walker's untimely death."

Underhill smirked. "The so-called Christmas Card Killer, am I right?"

Silence.

"It has to be," Underhill continued. "Criminal psychosis is a special interest of mine and it would be an absolute honour to study this killer, if you ever catch him." He had a wide smile.

I leaned forward again. "How do we not know that perhaps you've not taken your hobby to another level? Enter the mind of a killer by becoming the killer?"

The smile now faltered.

Kane joined in. "We will need to ascertain your whereabouts over the last two weeks Doctor Underhill."

His face almost shut down. "I have not left this place for nearly three weeks and have numerous colleagues who can vouch for me. I can assure that if you have come here expecting to find your killer then you have made a very large misjudgement sirs."

"Where do you live?" Kane pressed.

"I have a room here at the hospital," was the reply. "A lot of staff board here and we are also fed. The grounds and surrounding countryside offer ample walking opportunities for exercise and there is a pub a mile down the road in the village of Lunton,"

"So not even a trip into Southbury for some Christmas shopping?" Kane would not let go.

He shook his head. "I hate Christmas."

I studied him for a moment and could tell we were going down the wrong path. "How about anyone else that Miss Walker met when she was here. Did she make friends with any off the other patients?"

Underhill leaned across, relaxing a little now the spotlight was off him. "I do believe she was close to one of the other patients. I recalled she would always walk with one of the male patients on exercise breaks. They were always deep in conversation."

"Surprised you allow them to mix," Kane sneered.

Underhill shook a finger at him. "Not all our patients are dangerous lunatics. Rest and recuperation is the best cure for many."

I arched an eyebrow. "Who was this other patient?"

Underhill jumped to his feet. "I will need to go and check so give me a few minutes." He left the room in quick order.

As we waited, I assured Kane that Doctor Underhill was not our man, which he glibly accepted.

Underhill returned within five minutes with another doctor, who was skinny and very tall. A beanpole of a man with a bald head and wearing thick black rimmed glassed. He was carrying a slim brown folder, tucked under his right arm.

"This is Doctor Willis, who specialises in shellshock," Underhill introduced him

Kane and I both nodded a greeting.

"Let me start by saying that I can confirm that Doctor Underhill has not left the hospital grounds for many weeks," Willis's voice boomed a speech so clearly prepared by his colleague.

I smirked. "We have eliminated Doctor Underhill from our list of suspects."

Kane coughed loudly, clearly irritated.

"What information do you have for us Doctor Willis?" I asked.

Willis squinted at me curiously and then held up his folder before opening it like he was about to make a major speech. "The patient that frequently conversed with Miss Walker was a man named Roy Wilcox. At the time he had been with us for nearly three years."

"Is he still a patient here?" Kane asked.

Willis shook his head. "He was discharged two weeks after Miss Walker."

"Just a minute," I held up a hand. "If you specialise in shellshock, is that what Roy Wilcox was being treated for? Was he in the army?"

Willis pushed his glasses back up his nose. "Yes and Yes."

I nodded. "Do you have a photograph of Wilcox?"

Willis swallowed hard. "It is a curious thing as there should be a photograph in the file but it seems to have disappeared."

I smiled. "That is a curious thing. Can you recall what Wilcox looked like?"

Willis nodded. "Tall, about six foot five, and wore a thick black moustache. He had black curly hair."

"Did he have a limp?" Kane asked.

Willis thought for a moment. "He had some shrapnel imbedded in his right leg which gave him rheumatism during damp weather. It would cause him to limp on occasion."

Kane looked straight at me and made a face. This was our man.

I turned back to Willis. "The final and most important question, do you know where we can find Wilcox?"

Willis took a deep breath. "Unfortunately not as he left no forwarding address, although….." Willis opened the folder and speed read a couple of letters.

We waited in silence, Underhill uncomfortably so as he stood squirming, anxious for us to be on our way.

Finally, Willis looked up and cleared his throat. "We do have the record of next of kin. For Roy Wilcox it is his aunt. One Edith Wilcox."

Kane jumped up and took the sheet of paper from Willis. He pulled out a notepad and wrote down the address shown for Edith Wilcox. I was already heading for the door as Kane handed the paper back to Willis. Kane thanked the two doctors for their help and scurried after me. Within minutes we were back in the Hornet and speeding towards an address on the Southbury Southside.

16

Edith Wilcox lived in small grey bungalow, the fourth down in a line of ten identical such bungalows. Each had a small garden to the front and all the gardens were clearly well kept, even through the ravages of winter. To the back of each bungalow was a small enclosed yard and then a high grass embankment with a line of fir trees at the top. Importantly there was nowhere for Roy Wilcox to flee should we be really lucky and find him at home with his aunt.

Kane led the way as he casually ambled up the short path and knocked twice on the door. We waited for a few minutes as someone audibly shuffled behind the oak front door. Finally the door opened slowly to reveal a grey haired old lady, stooping badly as she held on tightly to a wooden walking stick for support. She eyed us both suspiciously. "Have you come about Roy?"

After Kane presented his Police badge, Edith confirmed that her nephew was not in the bungalow and ushered us both into a small lounge which only had two wooden chairs. Edith removed some knitting from one of the chairs and slowly sat herself down. I signalled for Kane to take the other chair as I remained standing by the door, away from the roaring coal fire that was pumping out the heat of a furnace. Kane loosened his shirt collar and I could see a few beads of sweat already collecting on his forehead.

"So, what has Roy been up to?" Edith asked.

Kane smiled warmly. "We just need to talk to him about a few incidents over the last few weeks."

Talk about playing it down.

Edith studied Kane for a moment. "Is it to do with a girl?"

"What makes you say that?" I asked

She took a deep breath. "Roy is what you call unlucky in love. He gives his heart so willingly and then always takes his affection too far."

I shrugged. "Has there been a problem before?"

Edith mulled it over for a moment. "Quite a history but the most serious saw him go to jail. It was just after he returned from the war and he was courting a lovely young lass. Grace was her name. One evening he took Grace for a drink but they encountered some drunken yobs in the pub. One particular yob kept grabbing Grace and using the most obscene language. It just pushed Roy too far and according to eyewitnesses he set about the yob with such a fury. I heard that the lad did not leave hospital for some three months."

Kane made a face. "What happened to Roy?"

Edith frowned. "He went to jail for a year and of course Grace did not wait for him. She married a greengrocer by all accounts."

I gave a quick whistle.

Kane shook his head. "So, Roy is quite the fighter?"

Edith shrugged her little shoulders. "That was why the army was the best place for him. He is very brave but also very smart. They sent him behind enemy lines but he survived because he is so cunning."

I fixed her with the big eyes. "But he succumbed to shellshock. We know he spent time in Southbury Asylum."

She nodded. "Roy came to stay with me a few years ago. He had ended up sleeping rough and there was nobody else to turn to. My brother, his father, lives down by the coast but they are estranged. His mother died giving birth to him and he had no siblings. He was very quiet and spent a lot of time in his room but then I would find him sat on the floor in the corner of a room, his head in hands and screaming for the guns to stop. He willingly went to the Asylum."

"Did you hear from Roy whilst he was in the Asylum?" I asked.

Edith held back a sigh. "Not at first but then he began writing to me every week. He assured me that he was in a better place and then just over a year ago that bizarrely he had fallen in love. It was shortly before he left the asylum."

"Did he mention the girl's name?" Kane asked.

Edith reached over and picked up a large pile of letters, tied together with a silk bow. She undid the bow and put on a pair of glasses. "Here we are; her name was Stephanie!"

Silence, yet Kane and I already knew the name before it was spoken.

I made a face. "Did you know that Stephanie died?"

She nodded. "Roy came back to stay with me when he came out of the asylum. At first he was so happy but then just before last Christmas the girl was killed in a tragic accident. Roy was inconsolable. He hardly left his room and then as soon as Christmas was over he just packed his bag and left."

Kane swallowed. "Have you heard from him? Do you know where he is now?"

Edith took a breath and smiled. "I had not heard anything from him until a few weeks ago. I received a Christmas card." She pointed to a card sat on the mantle above the fire.

The scene was a Christmas tree with wrapped presents at its base next to a roaring fire, exactly the same as the card sent to Jim Johnson. I walked over and picked the card up. *Merry Christmas Auntie Edith, I'm doing fine, Love Roy* was inscribed inside. It was unmistakably the same writing I had seen in all the cards sent by the Christmas Card Killer.

I handed the card to Kane. As soon as he opened it and saw the writing he shot me a knowing look. We definitely had the right man.

I smiled at Edith. "Do you have any photographs of Roy?"

She nodded. "Just the one. It was taken the day before he left to fight for his country. I'll go and get it."

Once Edith had left the room, Kane came over and stood by me, clutching the card. "This photo is going to be between fifteen and twenty years old. Not sure it is going to help."

Before I could reply, Edith was back to present a dog-eared photograph. She handed it to me and Kane and I then looked at it together. It was quite badly faded under a brown tint. The picture was of a young man stood by the side of a road, wearing an oversized uniform and with a very severe haircut. He had a cheeky grin on his face and an overly confident glint in his eye. I imagined how quickly that exuberance would have faded once he reached the front line. He was destined to survive but at the cost of spending time in an asylum.

"He's only eighteen there," Edith commented as I continued to stare at the photograph.

Kane frowned. "You do not have anything more recent?"

She considered for a moment. "Sadly not."

I just kept staring at the young man in the photograph. There was something familiar about him and I just could not put my finger on it.

Kane sighed. "And you really have no idea where he is now?"

There was a brief hesitation. "I do not know where he is but there was something…"

"I'm listening," Kane muttered.

"Okay then," she took a deep breath. "When the Christmas Card was delivered, I just happened to look out of the window. The card had been delivered as the only post and without a stamp. I was therefore surprised to see a man in a postman's uniform walking down my path. He had his back to me but I could have sworn it was Roy."

"Are you sure?" Kane snapped.

She frowned. "I could not be totally certain but I did knock the window and he turned slightly. It was just enough to glimpse a moustache, just like the one the Roy has these days."

I felt a cold chill. "That's it, that's where I have seen this man. He's obviously older now, but it's that cheeky grin." I held the picture up to Kane. "Imagine a bushy moustache on his upper lip and a mop of curly hair"

Kane perused the photograph for a moment before looking up and staring at me. "It's the postman that was outside Jill Smith's house. He said his name was Richard Jones."

I nodded. "The same postman who keeps popping up everywhere we go."

Kane mulled it over. "You had it right all along Harry. We need to arrest the postman."

17

I drove to the nearest police box so that Kane could update McAldren on the latest development. We now knew the identity of the Christmas Card Killer; we just had to find him. Kane confirmed to McAldren that we would head for the Post Office Depot.

Twenty minutes later we were at the depot that was on the outskirts of Southbury, on the Westside. Kane flashed his badge until we were escorted to the office of the depot manager.

"I must believe that Richard Jones has got himself into some kind of trouble," Mister Bamford, the manager, stated haughtily. He was a large man, over six foot, with a portly frame, rosy cheeks and a large handlebar moustache. A man who obviously enjoyed life to the full. "It all adds up," he added.
Kane made a face. "All adds up? Did you already suspect him of wrongdoing?"

Bamford fiddled with a sheet of stamps as he thought for a moment. "He really kept himself to himself. He was in the army and still affected by the war as far as I could see. He was very quiet and tended not to mingle with the others. Then this morning he marched into my office and announced he was quitting. There was no previous notice of his intention but today he firmly stated he was leaving immediately. I paid what wages he was due and then he was gone. And now the police turn up. Whatever has he done?"

I shrugged. "What would you think?"

He shrugged back. "A robbery of some kind. Am I warm?"

Kane shook his head. "We would like to speak to Jones in conjunction with a series of recent murders."

Bamford's eyes widened in shock. "Not...not the Christmas Card Killer?"

Kane nodded. "You should know that Richard Jones is not his real name. It is actually Roy Wilcox. The main question now is do you know where our man lives?"

Bamford stood up and walked over to open his office door. "I'll check with Valerie, my secretary."

We could hear a mumbled conversation in the adjoining office as Bamford raised the question with Valerie. Kane sat impatiently, tapping his foot. Finally, Bamford returned.

Bamford grimaced. "It would seem that the file we held for Jones has mysteriously disappeared. However, Valerie mentioned that one of the lads bumped into Jones a couple of days ago as he came out of a house on Burnside Road, which is only a couple of blocks from here. She's gone to check with the lad now."

Kane reverted to his impatient foot tapping as we waited again. Thankfully we did not have to wait long as Valerie bought a young lad to the office.

"This is Ned Southgate," Bamford introduced the boy and confirmed we were a couple of police officers. Kane did not correct him.

Kane smiled thinly. "Ned, would you be able to show us where you saw Richard Jones on Burnside Road?"

Ned looked puzzled and nervous. "Yes, sure. What has he done?"

"We just need to talk to him," Kane stated.

There was a brief hesitation. "It's on the way home to my parents' house. Shall I take you there now?"

I stood up. "Let's go."

Bamford nodded his agreement and we made our way on foot down to Burnside Road, Ned leading the way. Ned did not utter a single word until we reached the house. It was a large grey Victorian terrace about midway down the road. The front yard was strewn with rubbish and junk. It resembled the sort of place you would find a rag and bone man. It was a three-storey building with filthy windows that were adorned by ragged net curtains.

"This is the place," Ned confirmed.

Kane thanked him for his help and told him to go back to work. Ned trudged back towards the depot, looking very relieved that he was no longer needed. I could imagine the scene back at the depot as the workforce gathered to share the gossip. Kane had purposely revealed the truth to Bamford just in case Wilcox showed his face again. It ensured some urgency in notifying the police.

"Do you think he's in there?" Kane asked

"Only one way to find out." I marched up the steps and rang the doorbell.

The door was answered, after a good five minutes, by a short scruffy bloke. He wore oil-stained, I think, brown trousers, a very off-white shirt and a frayed brown waistcoat. He was balding with very fine grey hair and had coarse brown stubble on his chin. He just greeted us with a grunt.

Kane flashed his badge again and explained we were looking for Richard Jones, but who may also go be the name of Roy Wilcox.

Stubble Face rolled his eyes. "Richard Jones is one of my lodgers but he's out at the moment."

Kane and I shared a glance. "We need to see his room," Kane confirmed.

Stubble Face nodded and moved back inside. "I'll fetch the key."

I looked at Kane and shrugged. "I guess he's used to the police just showing up to see his lodgers."
Kane smirked.

Stubble Face led us up one flight of creaky stairs to a landing strewn with rubbish. A very fat man came out of his room to see who was about. He was clutching a bottle of Scotch and wearing a white vest that only stretched to just above his naval.

Stubble Face ignored his fat tenant and walked on down to a door at the end of the landing. He pulled out a large bunch of keys, opened the door and beckoned us to go in. "Shut the door when you leave gentlemen," he grunted and turned on his heels. "They're police Sam, just go back inside," Stubble Face updated the fat man as he went past.

I followed Kane into the room. It was very basic with a single wrought iron bed by the window, a brown wardrobe in one corner and a small sink in the other. There was a small round threadbare rug by the end of the bed next to a wooden chair. Moth-eaten net curtains hung in the window.

The room was so sparse that I instinctively headed to the wardrobe and opened the doors. I blew out a loud whistle at what I saw and opened the doors wide. Kane came alongside me and held up his hands in surrender. "Wilcox is our man alright!"

On the door to the left, a number of newspaper clippings had been pinned under a photograph of a smiling young woman. The clippings all covered the same event; the unfortunate death of Stephanie Walker. The photograph was of Stephanie herself. She looked so pretty, with beautiful jet-black curly hair, but with those piercing large brown eyes. She looked full of life. On the door to the right were five more photographs with scribbled notes written underneath, on the wood. I recognised every photograph: *Jill Smith, Peter Freeman, Lily Hutchins, Jim Johnson and….Maria Donatella.*

Under *Jill Smith;* **the Nurse who failed her**

Under *Peter Freeman;* **the man who broke her heart**

Under *Lily Hutchens;* **the Teacher who did not believe in her**

Under *Jim Johnson,* **the Bobbie who would not give her a chance**

Finally under *Maria Donatella;* **the bitch who ruined her career, to meet the same end**

Kane shook his head. "At least he tells us why he killed each of his victims. It comes down to how each of them wronged Stephanie Walker."

I made a face. "It is as if he has traced Stephanie's demise back to all those who wronged her in life. The pivotal moments that created the demons that destroyed her."

Kane leaned forward to read the notes again. "We now know who the final victim will be, but I think you already knew that before we got here Harry."

I took a big breath. "Alright I'll come clean. Maria contacted me because she has received a dreaded card. The problem is that Smooth will not have the police sniffing around The Blue Bay."

He looked up at me, some anger in his eyes. "So now what?"

I thought for a moment. "We go to The Blue Bay, just the two of us. We tell McAldren we're working on a hunch but there's no point is swarming the place with uniforms. We need to draw Wilcox out and somehow keep Smooth onside at the same time."

Kane pondered for a moment and I could tell it did not sit comfortably with him. "Lead the way," he finally conceded.

We jogged back to the Hornet and I then drove at top speed towards The Blue Bay. All the time thinking, what if we were too late? But surely Smooth would protect Maria at all costs.

I could tell Kane was very tense about the whole situation as he spoke very little. Finally, "we really should tell McAldren. He's going to go crazy."

"Trust me, I'll take the flack." I tried to sound reassuring.

"What about Smooth?" Kane snapped. "How are you going to play it with Southbury's most notorious gangster?"

"Trust me," I repeated.

Dusk was just starting to creep in when we arrived at The Blue Bay. Kane went off to make his call to McAldren. I lit a cigarette and waited as patiently as I could. I half-expected Kane to blab to the Inspector and he did look quite sheepish on his return. Apparently McAldren was far from happy, having made no progress with Peter Walker. He grilled Kane on whatever the hunch was and promised that he would give it to his young constable with both barrels if there was no progress. Apparently, the waste-of-space PI Banner would also get the same. Kane was asked to pass on the message.

I smiled, picturing McAldren losing his rag and bursting a few blood vessels in the process. "Let's go and break the news to Smooth then."

I stubbed out my cigarette and marched into The Blue Bay foyer with Kane several steps behind. We walked straight into the path of a couple of Smooth's goons, seemingly guarding the front of house. I did not recognise either of them, but then most of Smooth's goons tended to look the same from the close-shaved heads, thick necks, squat ugly features and ill-fitting black suits.

"What's your business?" the slightly taller goon grunted as he folded his arms and stood in our way.

"It's alright Bucks," shouted a familiar voice from the back of the room. "It's only a weasel PI known as Harry Banner."

I looked across to see my favourite goon, Marcus, grinning inanely.

"But just who is the little poodle you've brought with you Banner?" Marcus walked over, giving poor old Kane his most threatening filthy glare.

I smiled. "He's my assistant."

Marcus gave a disapproving scowl that was probably mirrored by Kane as he stood behind me.

"Where's Maria?" I asked impatiently.

Marcus looked upwards and rested his index finger on his lip. "Now let me think. Somewhere safe is all you need to know."

I rolled my eyes. "Glad to hear it but I need to speak to her, and Smooth."

Marcus put a hand on my shoulder. "And why would that be little man?"

"I need to see them now," I said through my teeth.

Marcus now squeezed my shoulder, hard. "It is not going to happen but I'll let Smooth know you called in, with your poodle."

I took a step back, shrugging the hand from my shoulder. The clock was ticking and Marcus was not going to relent. "Well I asked nicely so why don't you pop along and tell your boss that the police are here."

Marcus frowned." I don't think so Banner."

"I think so," Kane took the prompt and held up his badge. "I suggest you do as Harry says."

Marcus studied the badge and after an angry sigh said, "I'll let him know. Wait here."

Marcus walked away before turning back and making the shape of a gun with his hand. He pointed the hand at me and pretended to fire. The other two goons stood firm, with their arms folded across their chests.

"Don't worry it will be alright," I semi-whispered to Kane as re-assurance. I could tell he was nervous.

A few minutes later Marcus returned, smirking from ear-to-ear. "Follow me Banner, and you poodle."

The two goons stepped aside and so we walked through to follow Marcus up to Smooth's office. Another two goons, who I had never seen before, stood outside Smooth's office. Both gave me the daggers. Marcus opened the door and beckoned for me to go in. "Poodle, you wait outside," he barked at Kane.

I walked in and Marcus came in behind me, shutting the door with a loud bang. As soon as the door closed, Smooth was on me. He grabbed me by the lapels of my jacket and threw me up hard against the wall. He pushed his face in until we were nose-to-nose.

"What did you not understand about bringing Rozzers here?" Smooth snarled.

"I had no choice Smooth," I replied. "Hear me out."

I could hear Marcus chuckling just before Smooth threw a sharp punch into my gut. The pain shot threw my whole body and I went down to the floor as Smooth stepped back. "You've got two minutes Banner."

I was winded and tried to catch my breath. "Kane has been assigned to work with me on the case. He is the only Rozzer that knows about the threat to Maria."

Marcus laughed out loud, hoping Smooth would soon give the cue for him to give me a proper beating.

"Why did you tell him?" Smooth snapped.

I climbed slowly to my feet, still winded. "I didn't tell him. We found out who the killer was and went to his digs. Pictures of all the victims were pinned up, including the one he intends to kill last." I reached inside my jacket and pulled out the grainy photograph of Maria that Wilcox had pinned on the wardrobe door. I handed it to Smooth, "he's coming after Maria tonight Smooth."

Smooth took the photograph and scowled. Marcus stopped chuckling.

Smooth shook his head. "Do you have a photograph of this nutter?"

"Nothing recent," I confirmed, "but I know what he looks like."

"You mean you've met him," Smooth interrupted.

"Yes..." I started, stopped. "We've only just identified him as the Christmas Card Killer."

"Who is he?" Smooth lit his customary cigar.

"His name is Roy Wilcox," I replied. "He's been working as a postman under an alias. He's tall with black curly hair and has a moustache. He also occasionally limps."

"Limps," Smooth scoffed. "Well good luck to him if he can get passed the muscle I've put in place." He drew hard on the cigar and blew out a thick plume of smoke.

I nodded. "I could see you've beefed up the number of goons out there. A lot of new faces."

Smooth stared right at me. "I pulled in a few favours and a put the word out for some hired muscle. Cost me a fair whack, but it means the nutter won't get within a yard of Maria."

I made a face. "Where is Maria now?"

Smooth grinned. "Somewhere very safe, with two guards on her door at all times. So I suggest you go and find this nutter and then we can all get back to normal". Smooth gestured towards the door and Marcus duly opened for my cue to leave.

I got to the door when I was suddenly hit by a worrying thought. "Smooth, did you hire your new goons directly from the street?"

Smooth puffed hard on his cigar, clearly irritated. "Yes, and they were all personally vetted by Marcus. Are you suggesting they're not up to the job?"

I grimaced. "No, I'm more concerned that Wilcox might have infiltrated your recruitment drive."

"What are you talking about?" Smooth snapped.

I shrugged. "Do any of your new goons fit Wilcox's description?"

Smooth looked over at Marcus for an answer.

Marcus mopped his brow. "Not to my knowledge boss, although....."

Smooth walked over to Marcus and blew smoke right in his face. "Although what?"

"Although, we did take on this one bloke," Marcus's voice cracked so he paused to regain his composure. "He was ex-Army and very capable. He was certainly tall, over six foot five, and with black curly hair. I did notice he had a limp but he didn't have a moustache."

"Where is he now?" I snapped.

Marcus grimaced. "As the guy looked so menacing we put him on the door to guard Maria."

Smooth instantly barged past Marcus and beckoned for him to follow, along with the two goons on the door. I followed in hot pursuit, telling Kane to also follow. Smooth led us up a couple of flights of stairs to an old dressing room. There were no guards on the door. Smooth charged straight into the room and we all followed. A goon was laid out on the floor, out for the count. Smooth screamed out in anger and as he did so I noticed a white handkerchief on the arm of the room's solitary chair. I instinctively picked it up and got a whiff of something. I bought it closer to my nose and confirmed, "chloroform!"

Kane swallowed. "So, he's taken her, but why not just kill her on the spot like the others?"

Smooth spun toward him. "Be grateful he did not kill her, although what is sure is that this man will breathe his last tonight."

Before Kane could react, I jumped in. "We need to move and move fast. I think I know where he's taken her."

Smooth now spun toward me. "Where Banner?"

I took a deep breath. "When we went to Wilcox's digs he had written messages against each victim's photograph. For the four that had already been killed, the messages described how each had wronged the love of his life, Stephanie Walker."

"It was the same for Maria," Kane interjected, "*the bitch who ruined her career* if I recall correctly."

Smooth looked like he was going to punch Kane just for saying the words.

I took another deep breath. "That's right but he also added *to meet the same end.* I did not think much of it at the time but I now think he might have unexpectedly left a clue. A clue that is our only chance to save Maria."

Kane closed his eyes and nodded. "You're right."

Smooth almost growled. "So what?"

I started heading for the door. "If I'm right he's taking Maria to die at the same spot where Stephanie Walker met her end. The tram intersection on the High Street."

Kane followed me as I left the room with Smooth and his goons just a few steps behind. I started to run and so did the others.
"You'd better be right about this," Smooth yelled.

"It is our only shot," I shouted back, knowing full well that the stakes were so high and as for the consequences of being wrong ….

I led Kane back to the Hornet in quick time as Smooth and his goons split into two black Bentley Speeds. With a screech or tyres we all set off for the High Street tram intersection, some fifteen minutes drive on any normal day but this was no normal day. I pushed hard on the accelerator and swung the Hornet down a narrow alley as Smooth's Bentleys veered down the main road. Kane gripped his seat so tightly that his knuckles went white, and he even yelped a little as I swerved to first narrowly miss a dozy pedestrian and then a static fruit stall. We made it through and came out onto Park Street and the main tram route. I hit the accelerator hard again and followed the tram line that would lead straight to the intersection.

I made the intersection in under ten minutes and parked the Hornet as soon as I could, outside a bookshop on a small side road. Kane followed as I jumped out of the car and ran over to the terminal. The whole place was buzzing with people. Christmas shoppers congregating with their bags of presents and festive fayre, ready to catch the tram home. My eyes darted around the scene, hoping to catch sight of Wilcox with the hapless Maria. I could see Kane was doing the same. We agreed to spread out amongst the crowd and search in earnest. It was like a Rugby scrum as I pushed my way through just as the bell sounded to announce the imminent arrival of the next tram. I tensed. This could be where Wilcox may strike.

The crowd began to jostle in anticipation of boarding this tram and not having to await the next. I took a few elbows to the ribs and the odd shove from behind as some thought I was trying to jump the queue. And then I saw him.

Wilcox was just a few yards to my left holding a limp Maria upright at the edge of the track. I could see she was out cold but nobody else was looking that closely. In the crowd they looked just like a couple. I pushed to get through but people blocked my path and even pushed back, desperate to stop me reaching the front. The tram had just arrived at the intersection, sounding its bell loudly. Wilcox prepared to make his move.

Instinctively I yelled, "bomb!" Then I just kept shouting the same word. Suddenly I felt some space around me as people began to disperse. I yelled even louder as the path opened up before me. The tram was nearly at the terminal. I had space to move quickly and began to run towards Wilcox and Maria. The tram was nearly here and I was going to cut it so fine. Wilcox was suddenly alerted by the hubbub behind him and looked over his shoulder. He was startled to see me but remained unflustered. Wilcox pulled Maria's limp body up straight as the tram came towards them. I dashed through and he made his move, throwing Maria down on the track. Wilcox immediately bolted across the track to make his escape. The tram's bell chimed loudly as the brakes screeched.

I made it to the track and grabbed Maria roughly by the collar of her dress, dragging her to the other side just as the tram slowed to make its stop. It was in the nick of time bought by the fact that Wilcox had thrown Maria down a few seconds earlier than he would have wanted after spotting me in the crowd. Seconds that had saved Maria's life.

Kane had made his way around the back of the now stationary tram and came running towards me. I turned Maria on her back. She was still out cold and oblivious to the situation. I found a beating pulse and sighed with relief. I took off my coat and placed it gently under Maria's head. Kane knelt down next to me as people gawked from the tram. The driver had left his cabin and also came over to find out what was going on. Kane flashed his badge and told him to stay back. I looked down and spotted something pinned to Maria's dress. A Christmas card.

I picked the card up and read it out, "Finally number five meets the same end."

As soon as I finished speaking, Maria began to murmur as she slowly came to.

I gently stroked her cheek, "you're safe now."

Maria's eyes opened suddenly and she jolted upright with a start. "Where am I?" she whimpered.

Before I could answer, a loud familiar voice boomed from over my shoulder. "Banner, Kane what the hell is going on?"

Kane stood up to greet Inspector McAldren and thankfully took him to one side to explain the situation. The respite was very brief as within seconds I had Smooth stood over me, flanked by Marcus and another meathead goon.

Smooth let loose a deep breath, "is she alright Banner?"

I looked up and smiled, "she's doing fine." Slowly I helped Maria to her feet before getting Smooth to hold her up.

Smooth grimaced, "what about the lunatic who took her?"
I hesitated for a moment, thinking about what Wilcox would do next and where he may have gone. To ensure Maria's safety, I had to find him."

"Well?" Smooth growled impatiently.

"He got away," I confirmed but began to look around the crowds on the other side of the road. Such was Wilcox's arrogance, the question was whether he would stick around for a morbid confirmation that he had succeeded in his mission.

Smooth followed my gaze, "what are you looking for?"

It was then I spotted him. Wilcox was lurking at the back of a small group of workmen, craning his neck to see what was happening. I instantly barged past Smooth and began sprinting as fast as I could. I heard Smooth shout after me and then McAldren as well, but I had my eye on the prize. The majority of the crowd eyed me curiously as I rushed towards them but Wilcox was not one of them. As soon as he spotted me, Wilcox turned on his heels and fled. I screamed for the crowd to let me through and a gap quickly appeared as people rushed out of the way. I appeared beyond the crowd just in time to see Wilcox running towards Southbury Park. He looked over his shoulder and spotted me in pursuit before accidentally crashing into a man carrying a Christmas tree by the park entrance. The two men fell to the floor and the tree fell on top of Wilcox. It bought me a few seconds but Wilcox was quickly on his feet and running into the park. I charged by the hapless man who was picking up his tree whilst screaming obscenities after the fleeing Wilcox. For some reason I shouted, "sorry", before running into the park.

After I entered the park I immediately slowed down to walking pace as I was faced by a large crowd gathered on the main green. The people were listening to a brass band playing Christmas carols. I stood still and frantically looked around but could see no obvious sign of Wilcox. The crowd was spread across the whole green and some were frequenting food stalls dotted around the park perimeter. A waft of roasting chestnuts filled the air and I could see numerous children running around with gingerbread men or giant lollipops. The band finished their rendition of *God Rest Ye Merry Gentlemen* to a generous ripple of applause. Within a matter of seconds they were playing *Silent Night.*

I walked into the crowd keeping my eyes peeled for any obvious out-of-the-ordinary movement or for even just a chance sighting of Wilcox. I was in luck. There was a sudden commotion to my left as a woman fell to the floor. "You clumsy oaf," a loud gruff male voice shouted. And there he was…Wilcox. He must have been watching me from the cover of the crowd, waiting to slip away at the right moment. It would seem he had been watching too closely and walked straight into someone. Now his cover was blown.

Wilcox looked nervously in my direction before starting to run again, although now he seemed far more hindered by his limp. I immediately set off in pursuit and chased him towards a nearby chestnut seller. He ran around the side of the seller's metal trolley and just as I approached, Wilcox pushed the seller out of the way and pushed the trolley over to block my path. The trolley crashed loudly on the pathway as the seller screamed out in anger. The bags of chestnuts flew up in the air and a few chestnuts hit me on the head and chest. I was unbalanced but somehow managed to leap over the upturned trolley and keep running. Wilcox was slowing and within a few yards I was able to leap and rugby tackle him to the ground.

We both hit the ground near the bottom of a large oak tree. I was catapulted to one side and Wilcox fell face first into the mud. He was slow to react and I was able to jump back to my feet and get across to jump on top of him. Wilcox grunted and tried to resist but I pinned him down by sitting on his chest and holding firmly onto his wrists. We were now face to face.

I smiled widely. "You've made your final delivery postman."

Silence.

I took a deep breath. "Perhaps Stephanie Walker killed herself rather than face another day with you."

That got a reaction. Wilcox's face contorted in anger. "Don't ever speak her name in vain or I will slit your throat from ear-to-ear Banner."

I smiled again and goaded him. "Your only appointment now is with the gallows and you will hang without completing your list."

Wilcox's eyes narrowed. "You'd better kill me Banner if you want to make sure that the slag from The Blue Bay will not meet her end."

I leant in closer and whispered. "It would be far too easy Wilcox."

I heard shouting behind me and looked back to see Kane, McAldren and a number of Bobbies running over. I held on tight to Wilcox until I could hand him over. Two Bobbies pulled Wilcox to his feet and held him firmly. Wilcox offered no resistance.

I looked smugly at McAldren, "My present to you Inspector, one Christmas Card Killer."

As we walked back towards the park entrance, McAldren walked several steps in front, muttering to himself. Kane kept patting me on the back and flashing a very satisfied smile. A few paces behind, two burly Bobbies had a firm grip on Wilcox, who was now keeping shtum and seemingly resigned to his fate. The brass band were still playing; a rendition of *Away in a Manger*. Many of the crowd looked on curiously as Wilcox was led away but soon returned to enjoying the festive revelry.

Back at the Tram Intersection the police were out in force, holding back the crowds that had gathered to catch a tram only to find all services suspended. Several police cars were parked across the tramway. It was then I spotted Maria, still being consoled by Smooth. There was no sign of his goons. I guessed with all the police around that Smooth had told them to make themselves scarce. As we came up close I could see that Maria was very tearful and still in shock. Smooth looked angrily over my shoulder, towards Wilcox. Instinctively I glanced back to see Wilcox grinning broadly. He was pushed towards a waiting police car and I thought it best that they got him inside and away in case Smooth decided to make a move. Suddenly there was a commotion but it was not Smooth making the move. Instead it was Wilcox, who had quickly and easily freed himself from his captors and I immediately noted there was no sign of any handcuffs. Wilcox sprinted hard and fast but not to flee. He headed straight for Maria. McAldren and Kane were taken by surprise and too slow to react. Smooth had the look of any angry guard dog, ready to bite. I bolted after Wilcox who ran straight up to Smooth and Maria and stood right in front of them, goading Smooth to make his move. Maria had taken a position behind Smooth. The big man could not resist and stepped forward to punch Wilcox. He threw the punch but Wilcox ducked in time and Smooth lurched forward as he hit nothing but air. Maria was now in the open and exposed for Wilcox to attack. I saw him pull a knife from inside his boot but before he could lunge I threw myself on top of him. We both hit the road and I fell at Maria's feet as she screamed. Wilcox was strong and was able to recover in an instant and he still had hold of the knife. He jumped to his feet and lunged for Maria again but in desperation I kicked out and caught him hard on the left knee. Wilcox buckled and fell on top of me, thankfully short of stabbing Maria. I heard McAldren bellowing as the hapless Bobbies pulled Wilcox off me and to his feet. Wilcox was screaming obscenities but now appeared properly shackled, with handcuffs applied in short order. There was no sign of the knife in his hand. Further Bobbies were required to restrain Smooth, who wanted retribution. And then all eyes turned to me. I tried to stand but felt a little woozy. Kane came running over and I heard Maria scream once more. I looked down to see the knife sticking out of my chest as blood soaked my white shirt and oozed a small puddle on the road. Then everything went dark.

Epilogue

They kept me in hospital right up to Christmas Eve. Apparently the wound was very deep and I lost a lot of blood that spilled so quickly onto the road on that fateful night. I was fortunate that Kane was a dab hand at first aid and applied the right amount of pressure to staunch the blood until the ambulance crew could tend to me. I was lucky there too as an ambulance was already at the intersection as a precaution after the incident with Wilcox and Maria had been reported. A lucky man all round.

Martin Warburton, the Mayor, was one of many hospital visitors over the time I was a patient. He turned up with a very generous cheque for my work in catching The Christmas Card Killer, along with a photographer and reporter from the Southbury Echo. I reluctantly agreed to a photograph with the mayor, although only after Kane had been summoned to be in the picture on my insistence. Kane and McAldren had only just been into see me as it happened, so the constable was already in the vicinity. It was worth it just to see McAldren bristling with envy as he watched the picture being taken. The report made the front page and was great publicity for Warburton ahead of the elections due in the spring.

I really made sure that Kane got due credit for being such a great partner in tracking down Wilcox. My tongue-in-cheek offer for Kane to become a P.I. and join my agency as a partner was made with McAldren in earshot. I got the famous McAldren scowl in reply but I am informed that Kane is up for promotion. Hopefully I will be able to officially toast his success when we meet for a pint over Christmas.

McAldren was hardly gracious in confirming my part in catching Wilcox. In fact he went to great lengths to point out all my shortcomings in solving the case and how I would never make a policeman. A fact that made me inwardly chortle as I drank the putrid hospital tea.

Wilcox himself was being held in solitary confinement in a padded cell. He was pleading diminished responsibility on the grounds of insanity to try and escape justice. A plea that would be readily rebuked and it was certain that Wilcox would face the gallows.

My other frequent visitor was Maria, who always brought food with her and would stay by my bedside for the whole visiting hour. I think that having someone to visit and tend to had helped Maria recover quickly from her own ordeal at the hands of Wilcox. On Maria's insistence I was to come to The Blue Bay on the evening of Christmas Eve, where a table had been booked in my name for the prestigious Southbury Christmas Ball.

I was still moving gingerly as I left the hospital but was happy to be driven home by a taxi courtesy of the mayor. It felt strange walking back into the office and I suddenly felt very alone, somehow lost. Southbury was preparing to celebrate Christmas, free of the threat of a killer who I had removed from the streets.

I chose a white dinner suit for the night of the Christmas Ball, complete with dress shirt and black bow tie. It had been a while since I had put on a bow tie and I could still feel the knife wound chaffing as I did so. I looked towards my beloved Lafayette but just knew it would be too much to pick her up for a good blow. How I wished I could.

"Merry Christmas Harry," Frank Kayley shouted from his shop doorway as I climbed into the taxi. I waved back to acknowledge.

The Taxi driver never stopped yapping all the way to The Blue Bay. The Southbury Echo front page spread featuring yours truly with the mayor had brought notoriety. I was now Southbury's most famous PI, which was truly a great advertisement. The case book was full for the next two months.

I was actually relieved to arrive at The Blue Bay and get out of the taxi. The driver did not really want to charge me but I forced two ten shilling notes into his hand. I stood tall and straightened my tie as a nearby newspaper seller shouted loudly to sell the Southbury Echo. "Echo," he barked. "read all about how The Christmas Card Killer tried to kill Southbury's PI hero."

This was all too much. I walked into The Blue Bay where Maria was waiting to greet me. She was wearing a sparkling red dress, that had a split right up to her left thigh. Marcus was stood by her side, unsmiling and with his arms folded. Maria instantly marched over and hugged me. I grimaced as she brushed her arm against my wound, causing Maria to recoil. Instead she stood up on her toes and kissed me on the cheek. She left a large lipstick mark but I really did not care. Then Marcus stood forward but to my surprise he smiled broadly and then offered his hand for me to shake. I obliged.

Maria led me into the ballroom and to the best table in the house, right in front of the stage where the Big Band were just getting ready to play. The stage was heavily decorated with festive banners and balloons and to the right was the tallest Christmas tree I had ever seen. I sat down just as Smooth appeared with a magnum of Champagne. He actually smiled as he opened it and poured me a glass, as well as one for himself and Maria. He then placed the bottle in a large ice bucket.

"Plenty more where that came from Banner," Smooth said with a chuckle. "Merry Christmas," he held up his glass, prompting Maria and I to do the same. The Big Band started playing **Winter Wonderland.**

Tonight, I had truly found the spirit of Christmas.

Printed in Great Britain
by Amazon

73968778R00090